A Day in Deep Freeze

Conversation Pieces

A Small Paperback Series from Aqueduct Press
Subscriptions available: www.aqueductpress.com

About the Aqueduct Press
Conversation Pieces Series

The feminist engaged with sf is passionately interested in challenging the way things are, passionately determined to understand how everything works. It is my constant sense of our feminist-sf present as a grand conversation that enables me to trace its existence into the past and from there see its trajectory extending into our future. A genealogy for feminist sf would not constitute a chart depicting direct lineages but would offer us an ever-shifting, fluid mosaic, the individual tiles of which we will probably only ever partially access. What could be more in the spirit of feminist sf than to conceptualize a genealogy that explicitly manifests our own communities across not only space but also time?

Aqueduct's small paperback series, Conversation Pieces, aims to both document and facilitate the "grand conversation." The Conversation Pieces series presents a wide variety of texts, including short fiction (which may not always be sf and may not necessarily even be feminist), essays, speeches, manifestoes, poetry, interviews, correspondence, and group discussions. Many of the texts are reprinted material, but some are new. The grand conversation reaches at least as far back as Mary Shelley and extends, in our speculations and visions, into the continually-created future. In Jonathan Goldberg's words, "To look forward to the history that will be, one must look at and retell the history that has been told." And that is what Conversation Pieces is all about.

L. Timmel Duchamp

Jonathan Goldberg, "The History That Will Be" in Louise Fradenburg and Carla Freccero, eds., *Premodern Sexualities* (New York and London: Routledge, 1996)

Published by Aqueduct Press
PO Box 95787
Seattle, WA 98145-2787
www.aqueductpress.com

10 9 8 7 6 5 4 3 2 1
ISBN: 978-1-61976-083-7

Cover illustrations: Tombstone, © Can Stock Photo Inc / vician
Ice and tree blossoms photos by Lisa Shapter

Original Block Print of Mary Shelley by Justin Kempton:
www.writersmugs.com

Printed in the USA by Applied Digital Imaging

Conversation Pieces
Volume 46

A Day in Deep Freeze

by
Lisa Shapter

To the memory of poet Gil Pettigrew,
for all our conversations about prejudice.

6 a.m.

I woke up. It was utterly dark. I flailed around in my bunk wondering where the light had gone and bumped the warm skin of a back. I never brought anyone back to my bunk; I couldn't be seen with a lover, no matter who it was. Was this some boyfriend playing a prank on me? Had some shiftmate found my bunk closer to the door than his and fallen asleep here? I felt for the back and pushed at him.

A grunt.

"Where's the light?" I asked.

I looked around wildly. The bunkroom doorway, which had no door to close, should be directly to my left. Behind it the lights of the Factory's main room should always be on. I turned my head to the left and saw utter, total darkness. I couldn't hear any machines: not the half-felt hum of the generators, or the rush of fluid through pipes, or pumps struggling with paste, or the grumbling of pressure regulators as they added water, or the muffled clacks of valves inside the pipes. Not the faintest sound of any power anywhere in the Factory. That would be why the lights were out.

I looked at the figure asleep beside me; no, there was a little light, enough to tell the bedding from the blackness around it. I got out of bed and went to the window: the Factory had no windows. The Factory was three stories underground to prevent contamination of the town, the world, Above.

I opened the curtain and looked at the silent, snow-covered suburban street in the light of the street lamp on the corner. My street: my and my neighbors' cars were all parked in their driveways. The plow had been through, leaving icy heaps of snow at the street's margins. It was overcast and windless, with no sign of dawn or life. I looked back over my shoulder. A double bed, not a single bunk, and the sleeping figure was my wife.

I was Above; I'd been Above for eight years, a year longer than most of my fellow workers from the Factory, all men. I'd been part of an advance party of six that escaped one year earlier than the rest; we'd spent all of that year trying to free the rest through complaints, allegations, attempts at legal action, all futilely. We could take nothing with us; the company would have put us in jail if we had, and we had no cameras. We could not send an inspector or advocate in because of the quarantine. The company would permit only its own employees to enter, for safety reasons. It was our disgruntled and undocumented word against a trusted corporation whose chemical and pharmaceutical innovations had helped save the world from fascism. All the lawyers we spoke to asked for documentation and evidence; the most memorable ended our short consultation by shaking his head and saying we were asking the corporation to verify its own misdeeds.

After the first few months Under, all communications with the outside stopped. The one telephone was behind a locked door that no Shiftmanager's pass key opened. The town post office would not pick up the Factory's bin of letters since the smudges and damp stains seemed like contamination. "Dangerous goods that might be a risk to the health or safety of post office workers cannot be sent through the US Mail," our town postmaster said in the last piece of mail we received on top of a bin of unsent letters. There was no clean place Under; the drug was talcum-fine and turned any puddle or damp rag into slimy ochre mud. So our letters stopped going out long before we could have reported any trouble to any kind of agency or panel or board, or even our own parents or friends in town or in the towns around it.

I leaned on the cool wooden windowsill and looked out at what there was of the morning. Pressurized water and steam, high rail-less catwalks, open vats, sharp edges, exposed wires, and darkness—none of those was the real danger of the place. The real danger was inside each of us, even if the doctor that our old bosses had hired has insisted we could not "contaminate" anyone. The company's claims about "safety" astonished him: we were not radioactive; the drug we worked with was a chemical, not a living thing like a virus or bacteria. Our helper speculated that either the company knew something about its new psychiatric drug that it would not tell us or its concerns about safety were an exaggerated anxiety for its patents. Our factory had been a small pilot plant, an experiment.

Some of us grumbled that we had been the experiment. It was only grumbling. The drug came out of the company's work on drugs in warfare. It wasn't a battlefield chemical like mustard gas, or it should not be since that kind of weapon was banned in 1925. The drug came out of something smaller-scale and more specific. We hit a dead end there: we could find no information about who the company was talking to at P.O. Box 1142 in Fort Hunt, Virginia.

I felt the cold coming through the panes of the window glass. With a slight sound, the furnace came on, and the house filled with a soft warmth. The Factory had no climate control; it was always a level 55 degrees Fahrenheit, except under the sweltering evaporation lamps. I don't remember an entire day I felt warm there, but I had friends, boyfriends, blankets, work, idle moments to sun under the lamps… There were ways to warm up, and feeling chilled had been the least of my worries.

I got back into bed with my wife. A new mattress that we'd just turned, soft rich sheets, more than enough blankets (and more in the linen closet if I wanted them), a large plump pillow—and no danger, never any more danger, it was all over. I went back to sleep.

7:30 a.m.

I woke up to the electronic blat of the alarm, heart pounding, thinking for a moment that it was the Factory's shift bell and that I was late for work.

"Did I wake you up?" I asked.

"Hm," my wife Emily said around a thermometer, shaking her head. She was sitting up against the headboard watching the bedside clock and spent the next few moments fussing with the soft curlers under her pink nightcap and tucking dark loose ends of hair into place. I never understood how curlers did not pull her hair: it was important to her that she looked "just so" by breakfast; I would not notice one way or the other. After a moment she put the calendar on the bedside table and read the thermometer under the lamp. "Today's not good," she said.

"When will be?" I said, in my best approximation of cheer. I hated the feeling that I had to perform.

"In a few days," Emily said, looking tired and not at all in the frame of mind to be asked for something earlier and more spontaneous. I had no idea why she did not turn over and go back to sleep like any sensible person. I learned how to cook in the Factory, I did not need my wife to wake up early and make breakfast, with her and the house both looking ready for magazine photographers. Emily had given a startled laugh the one time I had suggested she sleep in while I do my own morning cooking and dishes. I forgot: in this world men cannot cook or do dishes.

"You're being a real trooper with this," I said, touching her shoulder.

"I wish the doctor could tell us what's wrong…."

I knew what was wrong. In seven years Above, almost none of us from the Factory had fathered children. The drug we worked with got into everything, permeated our bodies. If it could affect our brains, then it could go anywhere and interfere with anything. The doctor who'd agreed to help us could only shrug—the company claimed the drug and all its components were harmless, nearly without side-effects, but I had the sense that the doctor could lose his license for helping us and trying to study it without the blessing of the company that made it. He could only suggest we try to have children under more careful conditions, checking for this and that negative factor as we went. This year it was my wife: exams and blood tests and thermometers and calendars.

We both want children. I haven't told her about the Factory, or the drug. The doctor has said I should be honest, spare her the heartbreak of thinking we can conceive when very likely we cannot. My old Factory bosses, the men we elected from our numbers, who've led our investigation and fight against the company that did all of this to us, all the Shiftmanagers have said to me at one time or another that I should be honest with her.

The company has never been interested in finding us, not even those of us who escaped a year early, but the drug has helped so many people now that no one wants to hear what we went through or how it might be dangerous. We thought well of them, too, when we saw and heard their ads, growing up during the war; it was why we were glad to take jobs at their pilot plant, submit to intrusive physicals and questionnaires, and sign form after form. Now that we were Up, we saw that their ad men were still hard at work. The Factory's company had put its wartime good name behind a series of endorsements and advertisements for its new product: "a new drug of more use and help than any of the previous drugs," the "promise of turning psychiatry into a truly effective *medical* science." After all that, people who might have listened to a story of a company's mistake or a subcontractor's negligence now asked us what we had against progress. The current plants that make the drug have never had any industrial accidents or mishaps, or none that have made the news. But those plants had been completed, were far larger, and built on a different plan: according to news stories, the drug in them is carefully sealed away from those workers they never have to brush it off their morning toast or wipe it off a ladder before climbing it. The company's training literature for us said it was safe, so it took us nearly a year to connect the slick ubiquitous dust to our problems.

But our troubles have not stopped now that we are away from the drug. People in this city have heard of us: our first year Above we had one murder (with court case). Now we try to stay out of trouble and out of the newspapers. We do our best to blend in and keep our troubles to ourselves.

My wife squeezed me. "Emran, it's not your fault. You're a normal, healthy man; last year proved that. I don't doubt you." The doctor had agreed not to tell my wife about the drug or anything else that went with it. Emily ran her hand over my back, and her neatly painted nails made a sound against my nightshirt. "Oh, Emran, he's a good doctor. If there's any way we can have a baby, he'll find it."

"I know he will, Emily." I turned to her, made myself smile, then kissed her, careful to keep it a peck. "You just wait," I said, winking and nodding at the calendar.

I got up and took a shower. My hair was getting a little long; I liked being able to keep it cut. The Factory's cook had kept a careful eye on all the scissors (and knives and everything else similarly sharp or pointy), and getting a haircut meant asking him for a pair, then either finding somebody trustworthy to cut it or hacking it off, yourself, blind. I got my date book out of my jacket pocket and made a note to get a haircut. Emily came in with my ironed shirt and a matching tie. It was Monday: I shined my shoes, then finished getting dressed.

My wife met me in the kitchen, beautifully dressed in yellow and green with her hair done. Breakfast was on the table. My grandparents had a farm outside of town; for them a breakfast of eggs and Belgian waffles and sausage and a slice of berry or apple pie and a bowl of cereal with cream made sense. I thought about the doctor's advice and ate the soft-boiled eggs with a slice of toast and a glass of tomato juice, adding a waffle to spare Emily's feelings. My wife thought I expected big breakfasts and jumped to the conclusion that I was disappointed with her when I refused them. It's never occurred to her to blame me or ask questions. I was grateful for that. Every other ex-worker from the Factory has lost girlfriends, sometimes marriages, for not telling the truth. I had been lucky, but I must always be careful. I finished the waffle while Emily asked me what I wanted for dinner, and we talked about her plans for the day: vacuuming the living room, watering the plants (and were the violets in that pot gone for the world?), laundry, and what would I like to wear the rest of the week (did I have anything important coming up?), meals for the rest of the week, and she hoped to finish another strip on the afghan. Her friends would come pick her up for the few hours she put in at the clothing store, in town (to have a bit of extra money for the baby; normally she didn't need to work with the money I made), and remember that her church-friends were coming by to pick her up for bowling, that evening.

I finished the last of my toast and wished her luck. (I bit my tongue on asking her to say hi to Terry, an old coworker from the Factory who had taken up bowling in an effort to look more normal: to socialize with people other than our old coworkers and to seem interested in women. In truth, the man he had at home was someone who would never, ever leave him, a reciprocal feeling; the casual girlfriends they had were only for appearances.) My wife wished me the best for my day, I put on my coat and hat, and shoveled out the end of the driveway. The sun had come up; it was going to be a cold, overcast day. At least it was still and windless. I didn't mind the work; it helped keep me warm.

8:30 a.m.

I drove to work. The roads were as good as they could be with the weather we'd been having: a thin dry pack of sand and salt. Only warmer weather would melt the roads dry and clear—and salt-stained. It was a short drive to downtown Riverport, New Hampshire, from my suburban neighborhood. I pulled into my parking space, tried to smell the sea on the cold wind, then went inside, to a blast of dry heat and the smell of weak coffee. The secretaries greeted me, and I smiled back and went into my office to hang up my coat and hat. At least the weather wasn't bad enough for boots.

I went out to get the feel of the outer office—reading moods had meant everything in the Factory, the difference between safety and danger. With my first cup of coffee, I went up and down the office, watching and chatting. There was no danger here, just the file clerk, my boss, the secretaries, the delivery man, and a fellow from manufacturing. This building was just offices and files, typewriters and company exhibits, and a meeting room—safe, well-lit, painted, and carpeted. I had a nice office with a window, the door handsomely lettered with "Emran A. Greene, Accountant." I was still proud of that, proud that I'd paid back my Factory coworkers for the money they'd lent me from their since-Under jobs to go to school, proud I'd gone to school and done so well during the worst years of my life, proud of the jobs I'd gotten and kept until I was the accountant for this company, proud of the job I was doing here, of the raise I'd gotten, of the Christmas bonus I could expect, of the life it had allowed me to put together: the house, the car, the wife.

In all my days Under, I never thought I'd have any of it. I thought I'd be some man's, forever. The drug we worked with was full of nasty tricks. Above, it cured a broad spectrum of psychiatric conditions (putting a legion of resentful Analysts out of work). That was really a blessing, the drug's invention: I bet there's not a soul in this office who hasn't been helped by, or known someone who has been helped by, the drug. It helped with any kind of emotional condition: the death of a pet, anxiety about a surgery, a morbid fear of rodents.

Unfortunately, those of us who worked with it in the first pilot plant, all men, were exposed to something a bit different: it made us feel basal things, at random, toward anyone…and if two of us felt the same thing at the same time for long enough, then it connected those two men forever.

Sex worked. So did fear—and anger. The resulting bond between the two men looked like love. The men acted like it, hating to be separated; but I remember it, and it wasn't quite love. It wasn't the way I feel about my wife.

I took a gulp of coffee. The Factory's cook had made better coffee. He was murdered trying to fight off a rape.

I pushed the past out of my mind and started on the project my boss had asked me to finish by Wednesday. I had never thought I was especially smart in high school, or that I'd ever make a living from something that felt like a pleasant challenge. I might as well have had a job doing crossword puzzles. I went to work, my office door left open. I went in and out to ask for files, listened to the hum of polite voices, the footsteps on carpet, and the cheerful clatter and ding of typewriters. I began to make notes for the report I'd have one of the secretaries type up, strings of numbers and abbreviations that probably only I could read, with underlines, sentence fragments, ideas for how to phrase the report so it wouldn't anesthetize anyone who read it. I smiled at the clerk or secretary who brought in the files I requested or came to put them back. And about an hour later, I looked up and decided to stretch my legs.

10 a.m.

I looked out the window behind my desk, out onto Main street. The weather hadn't changed. It looked cold out there: I was glad to be in here and warm. I wondered how long it would take for me to get used to seasons after the Factory's constant level of light and temperature. I was glad, once again, for windows and freedom, and that put a smile on my face.

I walked up and down the office: the mood was still good. I nodded to the people who could spare a moment from their work or current errand. I noticed that one of the secretaries looked irritated, and one of the supervisors from manufacturing looked ready to tear someone a new orifice, but no danger to me or to anyone around me— and I remembered that I had an office to return to with a door that shut. (Almost no doorway in the Factory had a door hung on it, the whole place was half-finished. It had been built to be mechanized, not staffed by men. We never knew exactly why they put the 125 of us in that miserable place to begin with.) The morning had been safe so far and looked like it would continue to be. I circled around to the coffee station and thought about my options in peace.

I tried the tea: it wasn't any better than the coffee. It didn't have that pleasant drawing feeling, almost a tartness, that good tea has, just a heavy, dull taste on the back of my tongue. I'd almost recovered my full sense of taste and smell from having worked with the drug for two years;

even away from it, at first all I could smell or taste was it. I went back to my office and smiled (in a friendly way) at the secretaries, gave a bit of chocolate to the one who looked put out, said something kind to the file clerk (who was doing a very dull job with as much cheer as anyone could expect), told my boss of my morning's progress, and went back into my office with the tea, shutting the door.

I looked out the window again, never tired of it. The slightest cold breeze moved the dark twigs of the trees against the lines of the sidewalk. The brickwork around the trees was covered with dirty frozen snow and the concrete sidewalk was still a hazard of bare patches and ice, all scattered with sand. You could half-think you were walking in the beach in this weather, it was the same ochre sand as the local seashore. Not good for my shoes, not when mixed with rock salt.

With the overcast I was just able to see my reflection: I'd filled out and finished my growth in my eight years Above, eating better and not always worrying about the safety of my skin. I was starting to gain a bit of weight, had a husbandly, safe look about me that I thought suited my life very well. I didn't want to put on any more weight, though; I had a wife to please and my own self-respect to keep up. Just because I was safe shouldn't mean that I went all to seed.

I'd never understood my place in the Factory very well. I'd spent time there looking in the rare mirror trying to understand how I'd gotten into that fix. Some of us were fair game for everyone, some of us completely safe. You'd think the younger, the frailer, the slighter would make up all the boys, the victims, but build and looks—even personality—didn't explain it all. It was a strange alchemy of how we'd gotten along before the Factory, in boy scouts, high school, at summer jobs, and in regional sports teams, and how we settled in during the first months at the Factory.

All those factors determined who was a man, who was safe (and able to take the pickings of the boys).

The drug interfered with everything: our justice system, innocent friendships, our abilities to control our impulses, our affections and crushes. In our first days Above, the bond had blackmailed an Analyst into helping us (the fact that she was still working as an Analyst meant she was no friend of the company or its drug). She has asked us whether it was like prison, or war…but what she described to us of those circumstances didn't quite ring true. With the bond we could be paired up with anybody, permanently, by accident. With the drug the slightest boy could fly into such a rage that he could beat up and run off five of the burliest men Under; the strongest man could crumple into a heap of tears (or pitiable terror) at any moment, with no warning. Under was a very strange place, and we tried to make it safer by pretending there were two different kinds of people there, but we were all affected equally by the drug in just the same ways.

The boys took me for a boy: I didn't fight the drug or pretend it didn't exist, I was happy to have boyfriends (I was in my late teens, everyone there was between 16 and 23), and I was friendly to everyone. They caught on fairly quickly, though, that the men had also taken me for their own, and I was the only soul Under whom each side regarded as theirs. So long as they didn't catch me with one of my boyfriends, the men could dismiss the rest of my behavior as friendliness or teasing—I was asked to go on patrols of men looking for boys who had succumbed to the drug (no one would say men fell prey to the drug: anyone with a tendency to do so, for any reason, was forever after labeled a boy). I was also asked to participate in rapes, in public, with every eye watching the sincerity of my performance.

During those two years Under I got away with pretending as often as I could, I got away with saying I was bored or satisfied as often as I could (without harming my red-blooded reputation). I did my best to warn all the boys; but there was no way to undo the whole system, not while enough men insisted the drug was not a factor and that they could never feel a thing for the former classmates they.... When I was in an especially bad mood I tried to calculate which side got more: the boys who wanted a bit of fun with whomever caught their eye or the men who said they didn't want it but went looking, anyway.

With the drug, you see, there was no pretending: sex was sex, fear was fear, anger was anger, sadness was tears. It was flatly impossible to do someone you had no feelings for, a fact the boys celebrated among themselves and the men denied. Handling the drug made all of us too emotional, prone to outbursts—we still were and *always* have to watch ourselves, especially around normal people—but the boys hung on their boyfriends and said, "At least we're honest."

The men thought that was a taunt.

I escaped being raped, but that was no comfort when I had to look in the eye a friend I'd been forced to hurt the night before. I did the best good I could as a spy and a double-agent, but I couldn't take the whole system apart.

I finished my tea and sat down at my desk, getting out the papers for my next project and turning on my desk lamp.

The emergence of the bond had thrown everyone into a panic. It happened after nearly two years Under, obvious for everyone to see, and it took two men. They acted like lovebirds: one of them got his arm broken within the month. After years of casual dalliances the boys were charmed by the prospect of real love (or a man who could never bear to be more than an arm's length away); the men could not believe their eyes. Our bosses, the Shiftmanagers, moved the love-struck pair into hiding somewhere in the Factory and snuck food to them. Although we'd all tried (and given up) on escaping long ago, one of the lovebirds crossed the length of the Factory every night to creep up a ladder and try the combination lock on the delivery grate…no one knew for how long. Entire nights of worming his hand through the bars to dial "015, 016, 017" until he found the right one.

I wanted to pick up the phone and tell my wife to say hello to Terry. I owed him so much, I could never say thank you often enough for everything he'd done for me. But we never tell outsiders the complete truth about ourselves, not unless we've bonded them and all 118 of us (and our three outsiders) must agree to take any additional outsider in as one of our own. Right now the only other people Above who know everything about the Factory and the drug are Shiftmanager Sam's wife, one Analyst who still thinks the man she's with tricked her quite cruelly, and the doctor who needs to know everything about us if he is going to help.

They've all asked me to be honest with my wife—all the Shiftmanagers from the Factory, plus several of my old friends (and boyfriends). I cannot bond her, trying to get her pregnant is a terribly dangerous game (a thing she has no idea about) that rests on my trying to cultivate a wildly off sense of timing. If we enjoyed that—or any strong emotion—together, we would be bonded, and she would remember everything I remember, she will feel everything I've felt, and oh we will feel so much more in love than we do now. But the price is too terrible: I've been bonded.

I won't think about him. I have work to do. Any man who's bonded can go on about him (or rarely, her) for hours. I can't afford to think about him. I made myself find interest in my work until lunchtime.

12 p.m.

I patted my wallet happily and walked down the cold street to a place that had a soup and sandwich plate. I could afford anything I wanted on the menu, but a glass of water (slightly minerally, I liked the tap water here better than that of the Maine town I'd grown up in), a bowl of soup, and half a sandwich were all I wanted. I was a bit sorry when the waitress said all they had was minestrone, but it was a good lunch for a cold day.

I saw a familiar face through the busy mull of people on their lunch breaks and early holiday shoppers: a man a year or two younger than I with dark brown hair, calm eyes, neat (and often expressive) eyebrows, a straight nose, and a set of features that said "leading man" despite being windblown and somewhat red with cold. He was wearing a cheap knitted hat he'd probably borrowed from one of his boyfriends, the threadbare stuffing-leaking coat we'd bought him at a thrift store the first winter after the Factory, mismatched gloves, duckfoot boots, and a pair of heavy workman's pants that looked like they were cut for someone taller than him. At least he was wearing a full set of clothes: Under boys usually wore whatever was more-or-less-clean (or dry) or whatever they could borrow from a friend. We were all guys, no one noticed, except for the men who took it as another taunt. So he looked poor, and I pretended not to see him, as all ex-workers do, but he didn't pretend not to see me. He found his way to me through the light crowd.

I thought for a moment he was going to kiss me, the way all of us used to say hello in the Factory (and which, of course, we avoided in public now that we were Above). Worse, he was one of my old boyfriends, from whom a kiss meant something more than hello.

"Go away, Marcus," I said quietly, not looking at him.

His brown eyes danced. He was in a prankish mood, and my annoyance amused him.

"Are you coming to the company Christmas party?" He asked, matching my stride, in a pleasant but excited voice. He meant the great ingathering of all of us who'd worked Under; I'd skipped Thanksgiving. I tried to skip these events, in general: too many memories.

"My wife and I have plans," I said.

"Still trying to knock her up?" he said with an old lover's grin. His voice had settled into a nice singer-like quality that matched the handsomeness of his face. Not looking at him, he sounded a bit like Nat King Cole, and I missed the way he used to talk to me when the two of us were alone.

I clenched my hands in my pockets so I wouldn't push him away. I did my best not to swear at him. In this mood he'd only laugh; the more vulgar the swear the funnier it would be to him.

"Yes," I said, levelly, "my wife and I are still trying to start a family."

"You've got the—" a passing truck blotted out the exact word, "to do it, lover." He bumped against me suggestively, making it look like an accident caused by the uneven pavement.

"Was there anything else?" I asked, looking straight ahead.

"Oh, now, I've got a ring on me, too, Em. Where's your sense of humor, baby? Your chances are better—you weren't there as long—all of us are trying the same thing—that can—and seeing you—"

"I won't be attending," I said as civilly as I could. "Now please, I'm going to visit my wife—"

"She got a good one," he said, smiling privately at me. He patted me gently on the back and left in the opposite direction as I went into the fancy women's clothing store. Emily had just arrived, and she looked classy with her brown hair up and curled, her tasteful costume jewelry, and one of the outfits purchased here (with matching green shoes, bag, and hat). Makeup made her look prettier, younger, and I kissed her on the cheek. (A real, full kiss on the mouth might transfer the drug to her, might affect her, might make her more vulnerable to the bond if I ever made a mistake.) She said she'd finished most of her housework (except for working on the afghan), her friends were well, and there was some bit of news about a mutual acquaintance whom she knew better than I did, and my wife seemed (understandably) in a much better frame of mind than she had this morning. I smiled at her and wished her a good day at work. I squeezed her sea-green gloved hands, gave her another peck, then left for my own building.

1 p.m.

I was a few minutes late because of visiting my wife, but no one minded when I said why, and they smiled in reflection of my happiness. I was lucky I hadn't ended up with a man. There'd be no explaining that; sexual inversion was one of the things the drug is supposed to cure, I imagine. It wasn't something anyone ever talked about. Everyone in this building had a wife or a husband (as appropriate), everyone who's my age or older.

The mood was good, nothing to be wary of here, lunch always put everyone in a good frame of mind. I paused at the coffee machine. I felt a little logy, even after a light lunch; I just wanted to curl up in a warm armchair and doze. The Factory had had a sitting room with some books and an armchair (I willed down a blush at a memory, the room had a door that shut, and a boyfriend and I had taken advantage of that fact, and the armchair). I could nap, Under—unlike every other boy, I never had to worry about being surprised by a group of men.… But every single thing I did had to read the right way with each group of people. I had friendships I struggled to maintain, subtle points of etiquette I tried to keep to (or politely excuse myself from). I had no time to just be me, to take my eye off of who was around me and what they expected and wanted from me, not a minute in two years when I wasn't trying to put in a delicate, double-edged performance—except when I slept. But I had a dizzying whirl of obligations from the moment

I opened my eyes every morning in the Factory: messages to carry, spy reports to make, warnings to give, friends to apologize to, invitations to accept and decline, appearances to put in, facades to maintain, friends to socialize with in the correct manner, work my Shiftmanager asked me to do, and in every place but bed calculating who could see me and what I was supposed to look like in their sight.

"You could flip a coin," a sardonic voice suggested as I remained rooted in front of the coffee station, lost in unhappy memories. I looked around.

No one had spoken. No one was near. I grabbed the first coffee pot my hand came to, realized halfway back to my office that I'd poured myself a cup of plain hot water, and stalked back to grab a packet of tea.

I shut the door to my office a bit too forcefully.

"Shut up, Tarquin," I muttered under my breath. "You're dead: stay buried."

I could just imagine the reproachful, ironic look I'd get for saying that to him. The cast of his features meant he looked like he was always about to say something arch; I'd been surprised to find out how often he was sincere.

I uncapped my fountain pen and doodled with it pleasantly, enjoying how the line broadened and narrowed with the pressure I put on it.

"My Beloved is mine," I wrote neatly.

Where is your brother? His blood calls to me from the ground.

I shivered. There were reasons I didn't go to Bible study with my wife on Wednesday nights. The idea that I had waltzed through life, despite what I've done, when the Bible said rapists were covered with fire and brimstone, babies were granted or taken away (or withheld altogether) for the sins of their fathers, and the horrible eye of God was always able to see into men's' hearts.

I knew what that was like. I'd been able to see into Tarquin's heart, and he into mine. I knew what my wife would be able to see if I ever made the mistake of letting the two of us become bonded. Emily did not see what did not fit her idea of the shape of the world. I married her for that reason: if Marcus playfully gave me a kiss on the cheek, or my Shiftmanager put his arm around me because I looked sad, or someone said hello to me in a tone no two men from Above would use, then Emily would forget it, or not notice it to begin with, or dismiss my friend as strange or a jokester. I tested her by arranging a series of small, well-spaced slipups with different people whom she could not connect to my past with the Factory or the drug. I also tested her by mentioning certain passages from books or handing her certain newspaper articles—anything harmless and out-of-the-ordinary—saying, "Huh, that's strange." My wife-to-be always dismissed it, making a little face and setting it down, never asking why it had caught my interest or what she should notice about it. If she saw a second newspaper article or saw some mention of the topic on TV or heard about it from a friend, she became irritated and a little angry: there's a way the world should be, neat and orderly and sane. I liked that about her. I wanted to share that kind of life with her.

I wanted to forget about Quin.

Tarquin did not believe in set times for dinner; Tarquin served ice cream first, meatloaf and green beans later; Tarquin took me for walks and started a snowball fight or sat beside me in the shoreside park to watch the sun set or look for shooting stars. He picked the flowers from shrubs and weeds and wildflowers and came home with a handful that he put in a glass of water. He did chores in several-hour blocks about once a week when a certain type of mood came over him; the idea of constantly looking for a dish to wash or a surface to dust or sweep struck him as a neurotic waste of time. Everything got done in our little apartment: we did not fall into degeneracy or malnutrition, but we were both glad to be away from the Factory where everyone at times tried to pretend that imposed schedules, clear authority, and regimented order could lessen the chaos.

Everyone Under had their faith in order or regimen disappointed at one time or another: nothing could make the drug's effects predictable. Now that we're Above, perhaps after eight years some of the men still believe that there is normalcy or purity or order, that an ex-worker can do or believe something rigorously enough that he would never be taken over by the drug (and never has been). Men worshiped normalcy Under, some still did in their hearts; boys worshiped letting the Id take over.

The Id has no limits.

I never made much of church past a certain age, growing up. I'm only somewhat interested in it, now. But in general I try to avoid situations that might make me green and clammy with terror, the idea that I'd fall to my knees screaming "I did it!"—the drug makes keeping secrets very uncomfortable—overcome with remorse for breaking any number of the commandments, was a prospect I try to stay away from.

At least I had been faithful to Tarquin until death did us part, as I have been to Emily and intend to be, always.

I scratched out the phrase I'd written, then crumpled up the paper and threw it away, thinking in the back of my mind as I continued to work.

2 p.m.

Tarquin had been just another worker at the Factory, just another kid in high school and junior high, somewhat ahead of me, I think, with different interests. Although the boys had developed a similar sense of sarcasm and black humor to a high art, Under, Tarquin's look that he was always about to say something withering (and perhaps his inch of extra height) won him a place as a man. For all the time I spent among men, I didn't find anything unusual about him; I later found out that he'd taken one look at the terrible system coming into being around him and had decided to destroy it. He planted doubts, he made remarks, he carefully took lovers (not boyfriends), and with a very few other men tried to sow honesty, self-reflection, and not taking selfish advantage of anyone else, for any reason.

The Shiftmanagers were already doing those same things, for their own reasons. There weren't enough Shiftmanagers to rule by force, and they were just simply good guys. They wanted us to do as they asked because we liked and admired them, because we trusted them (and human intelligence and vigilance were the only things that found and sanded down the sharp edges, installed extra lights, added handrails, wrapped the wires, kept the place in repair, kept us from getting botulism, broke up rapes, and watched the gauges and indicators that could only warn of a pipe rupture, not prevent it). Despite everyone's best efforts, a pipe did rupture a month shy of the start of the fourth year

Under. It killed five, including a Shiftmanager. When the ex-workers who had tried to save my little cousin came Up a month later, they found me and asked if I wanted to know how he died. We'd just buried Quin that day. I didn't want to know the details, and I've never asked them.

My friends who were boys have teased me about the year I missed, and they've told me, without joking, that at least there were more boys (or at least men who had lost their status) by the last year Under. Some wish, in a way, that the place had gone on longer: when there were no more men then all the men would see the emptiness of having two statuses. I still remembered the feeling of looking for my little cousin's, my friends', and the cook's faces among the 113 who arrived Above—even after the Shiftmanagers had told me about the industrial accident and the cook's murder.

I wiped my eyes and changed it into a gesture of thinking when a secretary came in. She accepted my one-word answer to her question about my schedule and left.

I miss them to this day. I could not say goodbye to anyone before the six of us made the one and only escape from the Factory. Tarquin told me to meet him in the kitchen at the start of the dead shift, and then I was climbing a ladder with a bundle of supplies without the time to get anything else or wake anyone. Our advance party's plan fell apart: me, for example. In the seven years since we've all been Above my coworkers paid for me to become an accountant; but it's been no help in our efforts to investigate or get justice from the company.

At any rate, all our bosses had Under was our goodwill, and they used all the power we gave them to keep us as safe and as un-crazy as anyone could. I never knew if the good men were working with them: maybe that place was so dangerous that they couldn't even put a Shiftmanager wise to what they were up to.

As a good man, Tarquin managed not to rape, not to punish, not to hurt anyone, all while he kept face as a man. When the first bonded man discovered the lock combination, he had told only the Shiftmanagers…and the Shiftmanagers could not tell everyone because the Factory would blow up or flood (exposing our grandparents, our sisters, our parents, our aunts to the hell we'd been through). The Shiftmanagers decided that the discoverer, Terry, and his Beloved got to go, for their own protection. I'm not sure exactly why I got to leave early (perhaps to save my sanity?), and Tarquin got to go because of something he knew. (He died before he could ever tell it to anyone.)

I rubbed my forehead.

By then I'd gotten myself painted into a corner with my situation. Tarquin had lost his last lover to a boy, a near stranger who'd bonded the guy as his "protection." (After that, of course, the lover had no interest in Tarquin, a change that took place in a snap of the fingers and was total and irreversible.)

Tarquin looked around our small group of escapees, saw I was the only one available (and that I was wound up with anxiety and frustrated to the point of apoplexy). His proposition was kind, gentlemanly, genuine, and I said, "Hell, no!"

There wasn't anyone else either of us could turn to. We both understood the dangers the drug put between us and any ordinary lover. No one who'd come up with us was a possibility, so Quin and I waited, the frustration got worse, and crammed into a tiny apartment we fought about the prospect of becoming lovers. (Nothing either of us was intrinsically against, we'd both been with several men—and liked it—but point to a random coworker and ask if you'd like to abruptly be their roommate and sole erotic prospect.)

One day, in the middle of shouting at each other…it was like having an endless bucket of hot honeyed vanilla'd milk poured over you. We weren't mad at each other, anymore. The intensity of emotion had turned sweet, all of it, every emotion in our hearts pointed only toward one another.

We still fought about whether to have sex—but not for much longer. Why do that, when everything else we wanted rested in the other, when we trusted each other completely, when we spent every waking and sleeping moment possible within three feet of each other, when the one bed we slept in out of necessity became what it always should have been?

I didn't always love my wife like that; there were days I only liked her, there were a few days I hated her. The sex could never be the same: I could feel what he felt, the worst sex with him was always far better than the best sex with anyone else, man or woman.

I put the thought out of my mind. I started to write the report with half of my attention.

Quin and I fought a lot. The bond always wanted to go back to whatever emotion made it: the very lucky made a mistake with timing in bed. Some of us could see a movie and so long as they found the same things frightening or heartbreaking, they were set. Tarquin and I had to fight, really fight (not a tiff), had to get genuinely angry at each other to get that initial feeling back, to make it stronger, to have the love, loyalty, fidelity, and tenderness a permanent partnership thrives on. Normal ways worked, too; if we were kind and honest and sweet, that certainly helped…I don't want to make us sound like junkies. Of course it felt good to have that first moment back again, but the drug will dash you to pieces if you go without your Beloved, or that first experience, for too long. Many of us found it too sweet, too deep an oblivion, a somewhat dishonest way to freshen up a relationship and artificially smooth over its troubles—but the drug would also turn any one of us into a blubbering helpless wreck if we didn't give the bond what it wanted, quick enough. And all of us who were bonded were always making a wobbly balance between giving the bond so much that it would show us up to everyone, or giving it so little that it would do the same at the opposite extreme. There wasn't much privacy in the Factory, and most of us turned a mild blind eye to someone who obviously wanted to be left alone—but Above we couldn't have couples copulating on park benches or men in hysterics on the sidewalk.

4 p.m.

I shook off my thoughts and checked over my work for a half-hour; I could set the exact wording of the report tomorrow. I glanced out the window and thought about getting more tea, or coffee. I decided I couldn't stand either and settled for a cup of cold water. A faint roar and clatter rattled against the window as I came back into my office: a gust of wind, and some loose twigs and leaves were blown past my window. It was still overcast and almost dark. I sighed and shut my office door again, then locked it, then quietly opened the bottom drawer and took out a small box.

In it, wrapped in plastic, was a small square of tan cloth. I always argued with myself whether to touch or smell it, or whether to keep it wrapped up. We all wore uniforms, Under (why uniforms and not handrails is a question we hope our lawsuit will address). This was a square of cloth from Tarquin's uniform, a bit of the shirt, the last thing I had of him. (My square rested in his bony right hand, where I put it before we shut his coffin.)

I blinked at tears, not for him being dead, but for remembering. We were poor in that small apartment. It was drafty and thinly insulated, and we were never completely warm in the winter or cool when it was warmer. We watched every penny we spent on food, on clothing, on everything, and set every cent we could aside as we worked to find *some* way to free everyone who was still Under. (And, of course, to shut the Factory down permanently so no one would have to replace us. It is still running, mechanized as it originally should have been, under the streets of our home town. My worst nights were when I dreamed something had gone wrong and that there was no one there to stop it or warn the town Above.)

Tarquin and I did without: we had one set of sheets, we ate as modestly as we could, we didn't take the paper, and we went to the pictures all of twice (both comedies) in the almost-year we lived together.

All that money went to his funeral.

That day we buried Quin, we came home to find one of our fellow workers having a cup of coffee in a friend's kitchen, change from his bus fare in his hand, telling us the company had sent in a man and shut the Factory down. After nearly four years someone had arrived to let everyone out, with no word of thanks or explanation, saying only that it had been "long enough." It was almost five o'clock when the phone on my desk rang. I jumped, dropping the square of cloth, and snapped up the receiver.

"Hello, Emran," Sam said, with a voice like a good hug. Under, Sam had been one of the Shiftmanagers; now he ran a small restaurant where he employed those of us who couldn't keep (or reliably make it to) regular jobs.

"Hello, Sam." I smiled despite myself. Sam hadn't been my immediate boss, but he was a friendly guy whom I had always jumped to help (before he'd finished saying what kind of fish-scaling, toilet-cleaning, or drug-hazardous task he needed an extra man for). He had a way of coming by with a kind word, or extra help, or pitching in, himself, that made whatever he'd asked pleasantly bearable. "I can't make it to the Christmas party," I began, genuinely sorry.

"Marcus told me," he said, in a warm it's-alright-but-so-many-people-will-miss-you voice. I didn't feel guilty, but I did miss the faces and company of friends I hadn't seen in months—or years. Sam went on, "Emran, we're short-handed—"

"Sam…." I began to form an objection, even a lie.

"Do you have plans with your wife?" he asked. He's married and childless himself.

"No," I said, unable to lie to a Shiftmanager even after all this time. "But please, can't anyone else—" We avoided mentioning each other's names in public or letting any outsiders know about the experience that connected us.

"Emran, everyone else I could ask can't make it. I went through the list we all agreed upon, together, in order of willingness (or availability) to help, and I've come to your name. Please help, I can't do the end of the night with those I have on hand."

Our ability to work varied a great deal, thanks to the drug. Look at me: I've spent all day ruminating about the past and the dead. The drug makes us all moody—and sentimental.

I sighed, "I'll help, Sam. Can I please have dinner home with my wife?"

He agreed and let me go.

The restaurant would be closed and locked for the employees' dinner, the shades drawn, and for a little while it would be a lot like Under: male couples didn't have to pretend. Boys (and the men who've unwound now that we're Above) could flirt and joke, and we could all talk freely without lapsing into code and nicknames. It was a lot of fun if you had a Beloved (male or female), or if your lover was one of us to begin with…but it's a big reminder of Under for those of us who didn't want to live close to that world any longer. There was still a lot of camaraderie after working together Under and a sense of kinship from what we've all had in common while trying to adapt to life Above—but some of us have taken to normal life very differently from others.

I'm no pervert; I have a wife to go home to, and I love her very much.

I snapped up the square of cloth in its wrapper, stuffed it back into the box, then realized I'd hurt the box if I jammed the lid on. It was just paperboard, lined with white paper, with dark blue false crocodile on the outside, a gift box from some thing at some time, with a square of cotton wool on the bottom.

"I'm sorry Tarquin," I murmured as I put the cloth carefully back in the box, put the lid on square, and set it down in its drawer. I waited a moment, fighting tears. With the drug I could start crying—and then cry for hours, unaware of time or propriety or appointments. I would have to cry a little, at some point, or the drug would force that experience on me, but now wasn't the time (although the time would have to be soon).

I straightened my desk, shut and locked my desk's drawers, drew the curtains over the fully dark winter evening, got my coat and hat, and shut off the lights, locking the door behind me. I said goodnight to my boss, said his project would be done a day early, spoke to the secretary to expect my report, said goodnight to the coworkers still there, and drove home.

The car was cold. Even with the heater, the wonderful heater that blasted hot air the moment you turned the key, the car was cold. The pale leather seats had lost any hint of warmth from me or the sun, and the glossy dark paint on the outside hadn't absorbed anything from a sun that had been dimmer than a full moon at lunchtime. I shivered in my hat and coat. They were good, dense wool lined with satin (or very good acetate) from the men's clothing shop next to my wife's temporary workplace.

"They need to be warmed from the inside," a voice said.

I looked in the mirror to be very sure some vagrant (or an old coworker with a sense of humor) hadn't crept into my car. All the passenger seats were empty.

"Shut up, Tarquin." One of my old Factory coworkers had claimed to see ghosts all his life since he was small. I sometimes wished he were here, but I didn't know what would be more disquieting: the fact that ghosts were real and Tarquin was, somehow, really in this car with me—or that I was losing my mind, in a very ordinary way.

Then I'd have to take the drug to be cured, and that would make Quin laugh. I laughed too, a boy's laugh at things that aren't actually funny.

5 p.m.

I pulled into the driveway and rushed into the house. It was full of the furnace's still warmth. I kissed my wife on the cheek and she kissed mine. Emily took off her apron, set out the dinner we'd talked about that morning, and we ate, talking about our days. She'd put up her hair in a more casual way for bowling, a charming but less elegant look for her, and put on sensible shoes and a house dress. She was almost as slender as the day we married, and I was sorry having a baby would change that. I thanked her for the meal.

I missed cooking, I missed sharing the responsibilities of a household. My shift cooked when it was our turn in the Factory, I did my laundry by hand (including sheets) with soap and a steel tub whenever I could find any time, and I must have done a marathon's length of sweeping since the first task of any shift was always to sweep the slippery, powdery drug off of anything we were going to walk on or work with. Tarquin and I had kept house 50/50; it was only fair. I didn't see why the same shouldn't be true, here—the chores looked laughably easy after Under—but I could never think of a way to bring it up without telling my wife about Under or Quin.

Emily had a new joke, a rumor she'd heard about a local business owner, and a head of steam about a rude customer who'd come in late in the afternoon. I laughed, nodded, and sympathized, as appropriate.

I just said my day had been a quiet, productive one and that the tea (and coffee) hadn't gotten any better. Emily joked about sending me off with a thermos each morning (I laughed and praised her coffee and our brand of tea, which I really did like, well enough), but I really couldn't bring something like a thermos to work—I'd look like a road paver or a construction worker. I said that was a good idea: I could bring some of our tea bags to work in my coat pocket.

Under had given me taste for coffee, though—good coffee, so that everything worse is just a disappointment not worth finishing. I was always trying to recapture that experience: I'd always try the coffee hoping it was as good as the stuff the Factory's cook had made.

I helped Emily clear the table, and she went to get her things for bowling. She called back to me, "Don't you dare touch those dishes," but I washed them while she was gone.

She looked in on her way out and said, "Emran, at least change your shirt," making a little face. In the homes she grew up in only her mother or her grandmothers washed the dishes while men drank at fraternal organization gatherings or in the living room. I never got a clear picture of what happened if men were not properly settled and came into the kitchen or what it meant if they took over women's work like feeding babies or walking children to school, but any joke about a man in an apron or a woman who had to work in a job that was not part of the war effort or to simply earn pin money upset my wife a lot. She did not ask questions about my life before we married; I returned the courtesy.

I reassured her with the small lie that I would only wash the cast iron pot. I smiled and said I hoped she had a good time tonight with her bowling friends.

I'd never been able to get another shirt during my second year Under. I learned to be careful with what I had: after the first year the Company's uniform supplier would only send us notes about order delays on that pattern or sizes being "out of stock." So I rolled up my dress shirt's sleeves while the cast iron pan, or rather the sink, slowly filled with soapy water. I knew how to be careful while washing an institution-sized sink full of pans and dishes, but I could see why Emily would be protective of an expensive dress shirt and tie.

"Sorry dear, just trying to be useful."

She rolled her eyes, "Some days I don't know how you got to be such a nelly—leave the dishwashing to me."

She left at the sound of her friends' car horn and the moment the door closed I turned the faucet on full to fill up the whole sink. Once the dishes were finished, I changed into clothes and shoes that could be messed up—Sam hadn't said what I'd be doing—and carefully put my work clothes in the laundry hamper and hung up the tie. Emily had no idea how careful I could be with clothes. New clothes that fit well (and wouldn't fall to bits) meant the world to me, even though I could afford to buy both of us all new clothes several times over.

I pulled on a thick, soft sweater, grabbed my good coat and a warmer hat, and went back out.

7 p.m.

God but it was cold. A steady, pitiless wind had picked up. The car had lost every ounce of heat. It started OK (thank goodness, really), but I drove all the way to Sam's restaurant in a shopping development out at the edge of town with the car's heater on full blast and never felt any warmer.

A warm light crept around the restaurant's drawn shades. I pulled around back and went in through the employee entrance. It smelled like chicken stew and fresh baking bread, and hot, newly-frosted chocolate cake—the kind where the icing pulls up parts of the cake and you have no choice but to eat the mistakes and start over with more frosting. I grinned.

The first person I met, Terry, had been the man to discover the combination to the lock that had kept us all prisoner, Under. I warmly kissed and hugged him—a real kiss. "I've been wanting to say 'thank you' to you, all day."

"Then visit us more often," his Beloved Adrian said, giving me a bear hug in welcome and another full kiss.

Terry smiled at me. A kind man with a round face and a figure like a gingerbread man, he never made anything of us treating him like a hero. The most he would ever do if we mentioned his bravery or his patience was smile, and he and his lover had never tried to find out who had attacked them. Most men would have made finding out who broke their (or their lover's) arm an immediate matter for inquest and retribution. Terry and his Beloved never held that over us, never asked for an apology, helped in the restaurant (when they could, after their day jobs), were at all the Christmas and Thanksgiving dinners and at all the restaurant business meetings, and did their best not to let us make heroes out of them. They have been very, very happy together and will talk to anyone who's having trouble navigating the bond.

I blinked at sentimental tears.

They were the first two men to be bonded, and here they are today, just as happy and in love as they were at that first moment, despite everything that's happened to all of us.

"I…." I tried to explain what had possessed me to stay away from these men and all my old friends.

Arms slid tantalizingly around my middle.

"I saved you some cake, baby," Marcus said in my ear.

"I saved you some carrot sticks," another old boyfriend teased, unbuttoning my coat and running an appreciative hand over my thickening middle.

It took me a while to take my coat off, for everyone I had to say hello to, for all the hugs and kisses and quick, friendly conversations. Everyone at the restaurant that night had been a friend or a lover (or both); everyone was someone I'd lent money to, or helped in a quarrel with a wife or a Beloved or a boyfriend; I'd had dinner with them, helped them set up house Above, helped them move, helped them cook Thanksgiving or Christmas dinners, cheered them up when they were glum, gone to their weddings, and placed friendly bets on which of us would become fathers first. I'd gone to high school with most of them, I knew many of their families, and we'd all suffered in similar ways when leaving the Factory didn't end our troubles with the drug.

I went back to hang up my coat and hat. They were too hot to wear inside. Here I was warm to the toes, and warm through my bones. I had a bit of cake and a cup of truly excellent coffee (made by Sam; if I was going to work, he wanted me awake). I happened to be sitting with the few men who'd been the group to make it out of the Factory a year early: Terry and his lover Adrian, Sam, Shelly (my shift's manager from the Factory who was here to help Sam keep an eye on things), and me (minus Tarquin, who isn't really gone). These were the men who had helped Quin and me move into our apartment; they'd lent us the sheets and pots and plates we lived off of; they'd helped us try to manage being bonded (something none of us yet understood very well); they'd been proud and happy to see the two of us in love (none of them hated inversion for its own sake), and they'd talked to us about our fights. The five of us buried Quin with our hands and Sam's shovel; we'd been the funeral party and Tarquin's first mourners. These were the men who had all smiled and teased when I began dating Emily (as they had with Shiftmanager Sam when he met his wife-to-be a little later), and they were all there at my and Emily's wedding.

They held me after I murdered Quin.

They all kept me from cutting my wrists, kept me out of jail (as much as possible), and gave me the strength to tell the court (and the papers) that Quin had been a terrible, brutal man who took all my money and kept me in his bed by force.

It was a lie, the last lie I swore I'd ever tell. Being around them, any of them (or anyone from Under) reminded me of all of it: of everything that had happened in the Factory that I had to do or witness, of losing Quin and then lying to make the man I'd loved and mourned sound worthy of murder, of spinning such a tale that no one would think of love or sexual inversion but that I'd been bizarrely taken hostage in a cruel and total way…and it reminded me of how the drug has warped every good thing I've tried to do.

Seeing them reminded me of the past: as a man, Under, I had to use my strength to be cruel; as a boy, I had to hide the very honesty and sexual freedom that defined me as a boy and that made the Factory bearable. They reminded me of living with Quin and being in love with him (they were all bonded now, Sam to his wife and Terry to his lover, and nothing is better in the world than being bonded). They reminded me of how it ended.

It all made me sick—that I was a pervert, a liar, a rapist, a failure, a murderer, a perjurer; that I loved a man (and I betrayed every man I loved: my friends by raping them, the men by not challenging our stupid system, the cook and my little cousin and the rest who died, for us not getting them out sooner, those of us who got out early by my putting them through a death and the court case)—and I betrayed Tarquin, who won't the hell leave me alone.

Now I'm trying to do right. Everything on the outside looked all right, no one would suspect me of the past I've had. I buried it with Quin. I swore that night when everyone was freed that I'd never be a pervert or a dupe or a liar, again. I could have taken another boyfriend, instead I was trying to have a good and a normal life, despite what the drug could still make me do.

Sam saw the off light in my eye and drew me off to some place quiet. He began to ask a few gentle questions, but the only thing that made me flinch was his asking me about how things were at home. Long experienced with getting men to talk about the root of their troubles, he tried to follow up on it.

"How are things with your wife?" he said, in his always warm and gentle voice.

"Fine," I said curtly, "we're trying to get pregnant."

"I know," the Shiftmanager said mildly; he and his wife had been trying to do the same for even longer, with no success. Oh, of course he knew about Emily and me: I'd told him.

"Um, really Sam, things are all right."

"Why were you turning a little green back there?" he asked, sitting down on a drum of some sort of dried foodstuff. He gestured for me to sit down. I didn't.

"I wasn't," I said.

The Shiftmanagers are very good at getting men to talk. The only thing that would stop the drug from forcing us to make a scene (over an absent Beloved or any kind of upset or mishap) was profound honesty. Anything less, and we would do something that makes how we're different very, very obvious to even the most inattentive outsider.

Sam watched me mildly, his long face lined early with care. Standing over him I could see where the streetlight picked up the first strands of gray in his red hair and the gold of his wedding ring. He waited quietly for whatever else I might have to say, utterly patient and gentle. Other Shiftmanagers would goad or wheedle one into talking; Sam applied an infinite and untiring kindness. Who wouldn't want to talk to a friend?

I started to pace as best I could in the aisle between the pantry's shelves. I didn't have anything to say to him, and the silence was getting on my nerves.

I'd known him—how long? I couldn't remember meeting him: I'd known him, and nearly everyone here, all my life. If he would just let me mind my own business: I was happy, there was nothing more to it. But I had to say something; he'd sit here until I wore a path into the concrete.

"Sam, you know I hate coming here. It reminds me of Under—and of Quin."

Shelly, the other Shiftmanager and my boss from Under, entered the pantry and came up to us. He'd overheard me.

"Most of us can adapt to that, Emran," he said in a weary but sympathetic, voice. "If you spent more time with us—"

I snapped around to look at him, "Shelly, I have a good life, I'm happy with it—for once. Don't plague me about it."

Sam smiled mildly and shook his head a little at the other Shiftmanager. He got up from his seat, touched my shoulder, and set me to work.

8 p.m.

Sam led me to the prep kitchen and had me chopping and peeling vegetables for salads, pizzas (if anyone wanted carrots, they could have them), sandwiches, or the ever-present minestrone soup and whichever other kind of soup we were making that week. It was easy work. Friends ducked in and out picking up bowls of finished vegetables, dropping off fresh ones to be cleaned and sorted, picking up used knives and bowls for washing, stopping by to say hello, or to thank us, or to say we were doing a good job, or to tease us about something. Marcus, my old boyfriend, washed the vegetables in a small steel sink on the other side of the room. He was cutting out the seeds, bruises, and stems so that my work would be that much easier. That was kind of him; it wasn't his job to do that much work. It was just like someone from the Factory to do that; his current romance ensured that he wasn't in any way still sweet on me. We all shared some kind of history with one another, dark or delightful, but we all looked out for each other and treated each other with a similar degree of warmth and care.

Marcus chattered. He was happy; he was still living in a boarding house full of fellow boys; he liked working here; he didn't seem to at all mind being poor, not having a car, eating the things here that were a day past (or were a bit more food than what we could feed the customers). He owned half a closet full of clothes, used the household's bedding, rugs, blankets, dishes, and towels (and for all I knew, razor)…I doubted what he owned outright could fill a medium-sized cardboard box. He was still full of mischief from this afternoon, naughty, teasing, his brown eyes alight. He was still fully in love with the one whose ring he wore. He was happy, and he wanted me to be happy, too—he kept teasing me, prodding at this and that aspect of my current life, joking about how well I had it now, trying to cheer me up and make me see the good of the life I'd chosen, who I was with and where I worked and how I was living.

The agitation I'd felt talking to Sam (and before) kept getting worse. I turned around to face my coworker.

"Shut up, you goddamned pervert!" I shouted, "Who are you to tell me about my wife and my house and our baby, when you'll never have *any* of those things! You don't know what love is, and you never goddamned will!"

The man who wore the match to Marcus's ring was a big sandy-haired fellow, a broad wall of a man, who escaped being a bully by having a long fuse on his temper. However, he was at Marcus's shoulder in an instant (I would be too if I could hear his thoughts—although more likely the man heard my voice chewing out his lover). Marcus chose his Beloved very well: the first thing you can say about him is that he's very protective of his lover.

"Emran, do you want to say that again?" the big man said, carefully moving between us so he would catch whatever lunge I made. There was the sound of Marcus deliberately putting down his knife and pushing it behind something on the counter top.

I didn't have time to think about what I was going to do next: there was a quick pain as someone twisted my wrist from behind so all my fingers flew open. The paring knife dropped to the floor, and there was a slight sound as a heavy shoe sole stepped on the blade.

I was being squeezed securely against someone's chest.

"I will break your arm if you hurt him," said the soft, certain voice of the man whose brutally broken arm had gotten all of us out of Under. Adrian raised his voice a little: "I've got a hold of him, Clem, he's not in a fit."

"Yet," Clemson murmured, giving me a man's disgusted look for falling under the drug's spell. He kept a careful watch on me from the prep sink, a few of his steps away, while Adrian held me still and pinned my wrist behind my back. He'd learned the hand-twisting thing from a friend who'd learned some kind of do-do in Japan.

Someone, a former boy, neatly ducked in to pick up the knives for washing, Clem pointed to where his lover had hidden his knife, and Adrian politely shifted his foot so the dishwasher could get at it. Marcus had left to get a Shiftmanager, and once they returned I was marched into the break room across from the pantry.

Sam sat me on the bed, put a bag of towel-wrapped ice on my wrist (something he was very used to doing Under), sat across from me in a lightweight aluminum folding chair, and looked at me, disappointed. He held out a thin metal cup and an aspirin.

"The one murder we had Under, Em, was with a pocket knife."

"I know." I'd heard the story from my coworkers and was well aware of the irony. "The cook was killed by the one knife he didn't keep an eye on."

"Your paring knife—"

"*I know*," I said, cutting off his warning.

"Emran, any fit of anger could make any one of us—"

"Fuck it, I *know*."

Sam waited quietly. "Be angry more often, in smaller doses. What's going on?"

"I'm not goddamned gonna tell you."

Sam waited. His expression did not change; there was a kind light in his eye and a slight, gentle smile. He'd heard worse Under, he'd had to take the brunt of all our feelings about the invisible company that never kept its promises and acted as our jailer and taskmaster. That is why, I suppose, it was so important that he was one of us, and that he was so tremendously kind a man.

"Can you go back to work?"

"No," I said. Under it did no good to answer from guilt—if you could work, you answered honestly; your shiftmates needed your help, and every able-bodied man in his right senses counted. "I'm really sorry, Sam. I think I can work—"

Sam looked at me for a long moment, then left, returning with Marcus. I expected my old boyfriend—one of many in case you think there was anything special between us— to look at me with a boy's inflexible silence of you-know-damn-well-what-you-did-wrong-now-apologize, but Marcus spoke first.

"I'm glad for everything you have, Em. You had an awful time Under, and a worse time Above. I have my own life now. I can't want anyone in the world but him," he said, rubbing the thin gold band on his ring finger with his other thumb. "We're bonded: I don't want anything more in the world than what I have. I would swear to you that I'm the richest and luckiest man Above."

I remembered that feeling; I had it when I was bonded to Quin.

"I'm *very* proud of what you've pulled off," he said in the warm and sincere voice of an old lover. "Going to school, pulling yourself up—but you have your life, and I have mine. I'm sure you love your wife in a way I'll never know."

I wanted to start crying again. Nothing he said made me happier about what I'd done. The house seemed empty, the car seemed empty, the choice to marry seemed foolish and hollow. I missed Quin. He had been the best thing in my

47

life: the best lover, the best roommate, the best companion, and the ideal friend.

I made myself not cry. Anger bubbled up: boys were master peacemakers, placators, go-betweens. My man's old pride from Under came up; he was just telling me this so I wouldn't turn him into a smear on the floor. He knew the bond was better than anything else, and he was just being smug about it, mocking me.

"There's nothing between us now, Em. We weren't very serious Under, anyway." He smiled. "But I am your friend. You don't have the bond to sprinkle glittering sunbeams over your life, you have an ordinary life, maybe the harder (and braver) choice. Do your very best to enjoy what you have, what you've worked so hard to get—appreciate that lovely woman you snagged and be glad of everything."

"I'm supposed to apologize to you."

"Yeah," he said, his eyes full of a merry, but ironic, light.

"I'm sorry, Marcus, being here reminds me of—"

"I don't think any of us can forget Under," he said in a deadly voice. "I don't think we should try." He took a steadying breath. "I also don't think we should cudgel ourselves or each other about what happened. I hope you learn that one day." He kissed me goodbye with a fond whispered "baby," something-or-other, and left. The sound of him tagging someone just outside the door, and his lover Clem came in.

"Well?" he rumbled.

"I'm sorry I threatened your boyfriend." That's a contemptuous thing to call someone's Beloved, or at least it was in the tone of voice I was using.

Clem looked at me like he was thinking of twisting my head off.

"You just apologized to him, and I hope you mentioned that. You threatened me with a knife, too. If this was Under I'd just get together a group of my friends…."

"Tarquin was one of them."

"That would spoil the threat," Clem mused. He went on, "But we all know now that that men stuff was bullshit. We were idiots to go around bullying and threatening and raping people, our old friends and classmates. I won't threaten you: just cough up that you did something stupid, just now."

"I'm sorry, Clem."

"Not half as sorry as I am that you killed my best friend. I could have used telling him about the rest of Under, I would have liked hearing from him what you did to help us in the year we were apart, and if you and he were hitched I would have appreciated talking to him about being a married man."

"I am a married man."

He tapped his ring on the side of the chair. "This isn't a promise, it's an inevitability. I've got to stay with that kid no matter what started it or how we get along. You have all kinds of things I can only dream of, like a choice—to get married to begin with, and to stay married." He shrugged. These were facts to him, not statements of unhappiness, "I would have liked having Quin around, he always listened to my troubles and said the right thing."

He did that for me, too.

Clem shrugged. "OK. You said you're sorry. Come on, back to task—after you tell the Shiftmanagers you're sorry for starting trouble."

Why did I make the choices that I did? I killed Tarquin by accident—I mean that. I was overcome with anger and blacked out. The drug put me into such a rage that I couldn't hear or see; it made me stronger than I had a right to be, and I beat my Beloved to death with the first thing that came to hand. But everything else I had a choice about: disowning Under, borrowing the money from my coworkers and going to school, dating women, getting married, building this whole life that didn't make me happy. It was just that the bond was better and sweeter than an ordinary life; that must be it. What I had with Quin was better after we got accidentally bonded, it….

I loved him from the start.

No, that's the bond's old influence, the bond makes it feel like any random stranger is the fated and inevitable love of your life. If I were to ever bond anyone again, I'd feel that way about them. I'd feel that way about my wife if I bonded her. No—then she would know the whole thing.

We passed Terry and Adrian in the kitchen, and I went to the man whose arm had been broken, who had been so open about the bond because no one in that state could help themselves, and I shouted, "You flaunted your disgusting perversion, fucking in public. You made it worse for all the boys, and deserved every blow from whatever man—or boy—gave you what you deserved for being such a disgusting vile shitpacking nancy."

"Then you weren't really watching us," Adrian replied mildly, not looking up until he'd finished tending a pot of soup. "And you don't know who broke my arm, do you?" he said, looking me in the eye.

I turned to Terry, who was working next to him. The sweet, mild man who had rescued us all, who had held me as I wept after Quin's death, and I shouted a notch louder, "And you're twice as perverted as he is, that man whose attentions you take. You're a freak of nature, an effeminate, pudding-bellied…."

"You should talk!" called the old lover who'd stroked my middle; he'd overheard me from the hallway. A small group of boys had gathered in the kitchen doorway at the prospect of trouble. They were grinning, not worried I might be shouting loud enough for the customers out front to hear.

"Yeah," Marcus said from next to him, "either your dick is getting shorter or you've been eating like a pregnant woman."

"Who's the nancy, here?" another old lover's voice said mockingly from behind them. "Terry, who has every right to be with the one man he's ever loved, or *you,* who slept with everyone but the Shiftmanagers?"

Marcus eyed me. "And maybe some of them, too." (The Shiftmanagers didn't take boyfriends.)

I went after them but found myself in the empty hallway at the very back of the restaurant (where none of the customers could hear my voice), alone. Clem plodded up behind me, never more than half a pace away. "You never slept with me," he said, in a mock-sulking tone. He grabbed the back half of my shirt collar in one hand. "Em, stop being an idiot, that was the oldest boy's trick in the book: the 'distract, taunt, and run.' Come on, we're still looking for the Shiftmanagers, and now you have more to say—are you sure you want to keep doing this?"

I tried to twist out of his grip. "Let go of me you boy-fucking eunuch! What you've got with that ass-trollop isn't love: love is patience, love is waiting, love is a choice. You're not in love, you're just steamed up with frustration because the drug puts everything in overdrive. You've been forced to settle with less, a life of nothing, a life of crap—"

Clem interrupted me. "Given how our bond started, when I wake up in bed each morning I do make a choice—a choice of how I'll treat him, and what I'll do with this," he said, lightly touching his heart with his left hand. "I think you and Quin did something similar. Your bond didn't start in flowers and roses, either, but you did fairly well with it and made it something good, didn't you?"

He led me toward the front of the restaurant, past the three boys who had taunted me, all standing in the room they had ducked into to avoid me.

"You seduced me, you tricked me, you manipulated me. I never wanted a one of you, but you coaxed and teased and played on my frustration…."

Marcus looked at me and sighed, weary and sincere. "Go home to your wife."

I took a breath for another bellow, and Clem pulled my ear against his mouth. "Don't chew out my husband," he said, putting my feet back on the floor. "You dingbat, never insult an old lover—they know all the embarrassing stories about you, the weird noises you make, all your funny habits. Insulting three of them is just stupid. You'll be lucky to get out of this with an awkward nickname tied to some story you'd rather everybody not know." His head swiveled around. "Ah, Shiftmanager."

He escorted me up to Sam, who had just come out of the pantry.

"He's here to apologize for starting trouble. I'm glad he's yelling, I'd rather yelling than a fit." Clem lowered his voice. "And he's close to one if he always sits on everything like this." He gave me a slight shake of warning that almost knocked me off my feet. "He's just been real cruel to everybody, including 'the Boys'" —he meant the couple who'd freed us from the Factory— "and my hubby."

Sam looked tired and concerned. He whistled, something that carried better in the Factory than shouting, and Shelly came back from the cash register to give me an anxious look. I didn't usually cause trouble.

Seeing the two Shiftmanagers just made me angrier.

"Why did you two morons take me out of that place to begin with! I could have stayed Under—I would have been fine—instead you stuck me in a little box with Quin, knowing I was frustrated out of my gourd and he was the only possible, available man Above; you took me away from all my friends—and my boyfriends—and you put me with that god-awful, sarcastic, angry, impossible ratbastard!

Knowing that filthy drug would hitch us up, one way or another. It was all inevitable, once you brought me here, all of this—if you'd only just goddamned let me alone from the start! This is all your faults!"

They both looked ready to tell me that they'd brought me Above because I'd been a week from being found out and buggered by every man Under for the crime of pretending to be a man when I was really a boy. They looked ready to tell me I was a week away from being killed by all the boys I'd had to rape to keep up appearances with the men. They looked ready to tell me I'd been a week away from going crackers from the whole ugly, untenable situation. Perhaps I had been: maybe all of that was true.

Coming Above had been an escape, a lucky early reprieve that none of my friends got—they had had to suffer another year Under with fewer bosses who were so busy keeping the Factory running as the drug's effects got worse (and then, a month from the end, dealing with the industrial accident) that everything else had to have less of their attentions.

My two bosses exchanged a look. At a voice from up front Shelly went back to the register to see to a customer. Clem kept a grip on my shirt.

"Emran, do you know why we brought you Above?" Sam asked, "do you remember—do you read the *New England Journal of Medicine*?"

"What?" I said.

"The article the doctor passed around, by Henry Beecher—" Sam saw the blank look on my face; I hadn't been to the recent meetings about the progress of our investigation and lawsuit. "Well, do you remember how we all had to do a paper in English?"

"What?" I said again.

"In senior year, in high school, the big paper?" he said, carefully and slowly.

"Sure… I got special permission to do Journalism instead of Literature. I did a paper on companies and governments and government agencies that tested things on unwilling people, children, the poor, people who couldn't complain…."

Sam nodded. "And we couldn't complain Under because everything we sent out went to the company that ran the place, and they supplied us with everything…and we were under quarantine so we couldn't get out."

"Yes," I said icily. I'd lived through all of this, too, and certainly had suffered more than my boss ever had.

"I'm not our lawyer, but I gather one of the critical parts of a lawsuit is explaining what laws cover what you're complaining about. Remember how we talked about this our first year Above? About what we were going to do once we had everyone Above and safe? We haven't had much use, yet, for your CPA, but it's just a matter of time; we'll get more documents out of the company. I see you haven't been to many of our meetings or gatherings recently, so maybe you don't know—but what you learned writing that paper was the seed for our lawsuit; it even gave us the idea that we could do something about what the Factory's company did to all of us. They'll get to answer for whether they were trying to test out the drug on us, its safety and its effects; they'll get to answer for keeping us prisoner, for working us every hour of the day and night, for unsafe conditions, for everyone who died—including your Quin. You've been the key to our getting our justice, all of us."

I just looked at him.

Sam's voice took on a tone of particular gentleness. "You have no idea how you've helped all of us." He paused and waited for the expression on my face to change; it didn't. His hand rested lightly on my shoulder. "Emran, nothing that's happened has been in vain, nothing's been futile. Go back to your good wife, your great job, and your safe, warm house," Sam said tenderly. "Absolutely delight in every piece of good fortune that comes your way and in every moment you're alive and Above: the past is over, the future will be even better than today. You haven't failed us. Let go of being angry at yourself. Go home and tell your wife you love her." He hugged me and gave me a full kiss goodbye. "And please, when you come here to help with the taxes, be in a better frame of mind."

He looked at Clem, who made a noise that he'd let go of me when he darned well wanted to and not earlier, no matter who asked him to. Sam called up the hallway that he'd be right there with whatever he'd come to the pantry to fetch, and he jogged towards the main kitchen, a can of something cradled in his elbow.

We were alone. Clem cleared his throat softly. "Did Quin ever tell you who his old lovers were?"

The anger was out of me, and I was just tired. "God, no," I said quietly, honestly. "I'm not sure I got around to naming my old boyfriends to him, either. It didn't matter after we were bonded."

Clem made a soft, sad sound in his throat.

"Then I expect he didn't want to tell you. Could you read his mind? I sometimes know what Marcus is thinking."

"Only after we were bonded, and after that, he only thought of me." That's the way the bond is.

Clem nodded. "He'd be so sick of you acting like an idiot. He tried really hard not to take that place out on anybody and not to let anybody else get away with the same." He took a shaky breath, "I asked about his body: they tell me he didn't try to fight you, that every mark on him was something you put there. Of course it's useless to fight somebody in a fit, especially if they have any kind of weapon, but I think he was trying to tell you one last thing while you were deaf with anger. So are all of us, now, and you still won't hear. Please listen before you hurt somebody else: yourself, your wife—one of us, some bystander. You've never gotten over who you've hurt already."

I pulled my shirt out of his loosened grip with a shrug and a turn.

"Well I've never hurt you, Clem, so stop telling me who I need to apologize to."

I put on my sweater, got my coat and hat, and walked out the door alone without saying goodbye to anyone, and got in my car. Clem watched me go from the restaurant's doorway, a sad look on his face like there was still something he wanted to tell me. I put it out of my mind.

I went to buy some flowers in town, ducking into a local grocer's just as they were closing up.

9 p.m.

The awful thing about New England winters is that they seem infinitely dark and cold. Once night sets in, it seems like it will be night, ever colder, forever. At least the wind had died down. I drove past the great brick Riverport Public Library, past the quiet clapboard churches and houses in the older part of town, passed the yellow-bricked Masonic meeting hall, and pulled up on the icy gravel next to the granite wall in a suburban neighborhood full of semi-Victorian houses far older than mine. I stepped over the chain meant to keep out cars and was happy the caretaker had done his job—if it was icy here it would be too dark to tell until you'd fallen.

I walked past the elaborate headstones of old family plots announcing this or that clergyman or town worthy's surname, down a slope past somewhat older individual stones and mausoleums, back along the road leading toward the original fenced-in plot where slate stones with strange epitaphs advertised our universal mortality with eerie carvings of skulls and willows. I walked back toward them, then veered right and went up another hill, stopping at a grave near the top. I didn't feel cold at all after the walk.

I had made it: I would always know where this grave was.

I sat down, careful to be off to one side of the occupant's waist, as one would sit on the bedside of a loved one.

I glanced around; everything looked neat and well kept. I think I will be buried here. One of the first things I did once I had money was to buy the plot next to it. I told my wife I'd inherited it and said we'd work out our own arrangements—but I'd never changed my will, and I've made my younger friends from Under promise that my last wishes will stick, no matter what my wife says.

"Why do you think you'll die first?" a sardonic voice asked.

"All of this is going to catch up with me, Quin: I have a date with a pistol, or some angry husband less patient than Clem—or any of us that gets too mad at something I say, so the drug takes over him, and—"

"You're more morbid than I am, and I'm the dead one," he said mordantly.

"I know, Quin." I sighed, setting down the flowers and touching the only epitaph under his name: *Beloved*. I felt warm.

The first thing he'd done when we were Above was tease me about my name, and I'd teased him about his. He never explained what his parents' fascination was with early Roman history. I suppose it was a little better than going through life called "Julius Caesar." I'd known his parents, growing up, the same way he knew mine, the same way most of us from our small town and the surrounding hamlets knew each other's parents and aunts and uncles and cousins.... Many of us were distantly related. I'd spent most of Under trying to protect my sixteen-year-old cousin who'd ended up getting killed in the accident. They were all buried back home. Most of us avoided our hometowns because all of those grandparents and uncles and mothers thought we *were* perverts, who all had no ambition between the lot of us and no gratitude about the company that had come into our town to lift it up by building a factory and giving us all good work, making something that would help people and change the world for good.

I wasn't in the least cold for sitting outside on a winter's night. Maybe I simply didn't care.

"Maybe I'm keeping you warm—and alive."

I patted the earth over his shoulder in reply.

One of the strangest things about Quin's death had been that our old coworker, the one who'd always said he could see ghosts, passed on a message to me from my Beloved from the beyond. Tarquin had said I'd marry and gave my wife's name. (Correctly.) He said we'd have a daughter, and then he gave her name. (My wife and I haven't started suggesting names, and I was certainly not going to mention that one.) And Tarquin had said there was something better waiting for me, a happier time in my life that only his death would let me have.

"This isn't it, Tarquin. This can't be the life you meant."

There was no sound but the rustle of dead leaves in an ancient tree across the hill. The wall cut off the wind; that must be why it felt warmer here. Of course, I didn't really mean I heard his voice. I was not crazy, and I didn't believe in ghosts. (Although the more delicate boys—or at least those who liked a good story—had claimed to see the Factory cook's ghost putting away spices at the restaurant or tskingly shaking his head over a sink of unwashed pots.) Stories. Our old coworker was just trying to console me over the death of my love, to console me about the inconsolable. No one else has ever lost a Beloved, no one among us can speak to how I felt or how it ended the bond but didn't.

I sighed.

"I've been really angry and cruel-hearted to men who've been nothing but kind to me. If they're ever my friends again, Quin, I'll be lucky. Luckier than I deserve. I've been sad all day—sad about you, sad about everything that's happened. Once again, Beloved, I'm sorry. I know that doesn't cover it, but I will say it every day for the rest of my life and still not get to how I feel." I cried for a while, regretting, missing, apologizing—all uselessly. "I brought you flowers, just as I promised. Peonies." I smiled at a memory.

I went on, "Clem says he misses you. I miss you too. We both wish we could talk to you—about this and that. He's with Marcus now, my old lay, or one of them...." Quin and I had joked about our pasts (we each knew we had them), but after we were bonded there was no chance that any man could be better than the one we each held in our arms. "Anyway, I wish you could help me sort this all out—everything is just OK: my wife, my job, the house we'll be paying off until...." I sighed. "Everything's gray as that sky you spent all day looking up at today." I patted the soil and stroked it as if he could feel my hand on his collarbone. "I know you're not cold, you're the temperature of the ground; I know that when I've dreamed about you—but I was cold all day, and everything's just so-so. Except at Sam's place, with everyone. And the only time I really feel anything is while I'm talking to you. Even when I was mad at all my friends.... They want me to be honest. I am being honest! I've never been more honest in my life: everything's out in the open, I'm not hiding anything, I'm as happy as I've ever been, I've got everything I could ever want. Not a damn thing's wrong and I feel great, goddamit." I shivered a little.

Of course it was always possible that Quin had meant some relationship after this one...and thinking over his words, again, they didn't rule out adoption. It wouldn't be nice of him to prophesy some cruel future divorce from some as-yet unmet wife when I was just bereaved. Tarquin had originally approached me as just something casual. We'd talked all along about how this wouldn't be permanent, a little thing to tide us over until the drug worked out of our systems, and I was one who resisted our becoming lovers. Our fights were my fault: sex had become a thing I had to do (for one reason or another) while Under. Either I had to stay in good with a boyfriend or look right to the men. It wasn't Quin's fault I'd been through that, or that sex had long since lost its pleasant, easy, nice qualities.

And he didn't insist, he waited and waited, asked only when I was obviously impatient—and it took the drug realigning every part of my being toward him for me to say yes. (I'd started out Under at first perfectly happy to sleep with anyone who caught my eye, and when the first thing I felt for Quin was attraction….) I'd already started to get it all wrong then, to be twisted around and lost from how I felt.

I was just being cold-hearted and stubborn—then and today—too wrapped up in my own troubles, too quick to lash out when all he was doing—all any of my friends tonight were doing—was being kind.

"I think that's all of it," I said, running my hand over the frost-stiff grass under the headstone. I should be chilled sitting out at night like this, but I wasn't at all. I smiled. "Enjoy the flowers, Beloved. I'll stick out being alive and hope things get better, like Sam said. Sleep well and don't come into my dreams. If I think you've crawled into my bunk, I'll say things that'll give the whole thing up to my wife," I got to my feet and started brushing off my coat, carefully. "Should I bond with her?"

"Do you want to know everything she thinks about you?"

That made me uneasy, and I shook my head in reply. I walked down the hill, along the road running under the shelter of the wall, stepped over the chain, shivered, dusted off my gloves, and got back into the car. My hands and face and feet were cold from being out in the weather. Dammit, I wouldn't be warm until morning—or spring.

10 p.m.

I shivered in the car most of the way home, feeling a little better when I pulled into my own driveway. At least it hadn't snowed or sleeted today; there wasn't any icy hump left by the plow that I'd have to break up now. That kind of thing became solid ice if left until morning. As I got out of the car I thought again about getting some kind of tarp to put over it to keep off the ice and any snow that fell overnight. I tried to remember the weather report and couldn't. Well, there wasn't any tarp that wouldn't look silly, as if I were building some half-finished thing in my own driveway. I fretted over the salt stains along the running boards, white against the car's dark glossy paint. Was it a deep blue? Or black? Or had it been green? I'd been so proud of the car when we'd bought it; now I couldn't quite tell (or remember) what color it was. In this light there was no telling; the light from behind the house didn't strike the paint directly. Whatever it was, the thrown-up salt and sand would just eat away at it and at the underside of the car. I'd have to get it washed—goddamn this was just never-ending. It would snow again, they'd salt again, or they'd salt just on principle to keep ice off the roads, and it'd start all over again.

When would it be spring?

I went into the house with a fatigued sigh. My wife was home. There was no sign of my visit to Tarquin on my shoes or coat or clothes: she could never learn about the Factory or the drug—or my Beloved. The earth in the graveyard was all winter-cold; any mud or dirt was frozen into solid shapes that wouldn't stick to my shoes until March—or later.

I took off my coat and hat, hung up my sweater, and went to kiss her on the cheek. She tried to kiss my mouth. I instinctively dodged, but let her—cautiously keeping my mouth shut and holding my breath so that the drug would have no way to pass from my body into hers. The first baby any one of us had fathered was stillborn, and we could only think it was because of the drug.

"How was your day, Em?" I said, trying to sound as sweet and concerned as I could. By now I just felt tired.

"You asked me that at dinner," she said with a little laugh.

"Then how was your evening?" I cranked a smile onto my face.

"You look dead tired—where were you? I thought you'd be here when I got home." She looked warm and content and sounded sweetly worried rather than angry.

I tried not to give a guilty start. "Didn't I tell you? My cousin Sam—you've met him—was shorthanded for the dinner rush."

"Em, you're too kind to him," she said. "You've worked all day today, only to go off and work another half-day?"

Sitting at a safe desk all day with an endless supply of coffee didn't seem to qualify as working, not by the Factory's standards, and what work I'd gotten done at Sam's wasn't any worse than helping out with any daily meal Under.

"I'm so sorry, Emily. We got busy, and I lost track of time. I didn't mean to leave you alone."

I hadn't thought of her once. I wondered if that mattered. If this had been Quin I was coming home to, his absence would have been a terrible gnawing ache within ten minutes of us parting. Was this normal? Does love feel like this? I don't feel like I love her.

If it were Quin, he would have gone to Sam's with me. If I'd made this home with Quin… I was going to start crying.

"You're right, Em, I am tired," I said quickly, "I'm going to take a hot shower to warm up."

"Isn't it warm in there, with the heat and all the ovens?" Her voice said at my back.

"The drive home was cold, remind me to ask them to check the car's heater next time we take it in," I called through the closed bathroom door as I took off my clothes.

The house's air felt warm against my skin, but I turned on the bathroom heater anyway and waited for the element to turn a pleasantly toasty orange. I rubbed my bare arms, firmly blinking back tears. Dammit, I feel like my bones are made of ice. How could I feel warm talking to my old Beloved, outside in the winter, and chilled to the bone while talking to my own wife in our comfortably heated house with a new furnace? I got into the shower and cried, trying to keep it under the noise of the water.

If Quin were alive this house would be even better—he'd be here, and he'd work, of course, so he and I could finally have everything we pleased. Not just things, but our whole lives together: I never got a chance to find out what he wanted to go to school in, or what he really wanted to do. We worked at Sam's, and at any small job in town, making just enough to put bread on the table, pay rent, and set aside every spare dime so our 113 coworkers would have something to start their lives with as soon as they arrived Above.

Tarquin had talked as though he'd disappointed me by our getting bonded, as though I'd really wanted an ordinary life with a wife and a house and kids.… I didn't want a different house, now, or any other woman as my wife, or a better car, or a different job. All of that was good, really. I have enjoyed it as much as I could, without Quin. But that other life, with him, with weeks of either bologna or pea-

nut butter sandwiches for lunch, that crummy, poor life…
it had been better than this ever had been, or could be.

11 p.m.

I cried until I could make myself stop. I knew I had better shut off the water if Emily was going to have any hot water left. I made a quick pretext at washing, shut off the water, made a brief foray at brushing my teeth, then changed in the bathroom so that I went to bed in full-length winter pajamas with wide satin cuffs, under a robe, with warm socks and slippers.

I'd slept naked next to Quin all through our winter together.

I imagined (I no longer knew what my lover was thinking) that Emily was out in the living room reading her library book. I settled into bed, glad of some time alone to think. I pulled up the covers—this was as close to a solitary armchair as I'd get these days—curled up, and shut my eyes. I wiggled my toes against the pleasantly soft wool of the socks: the first item of clothing to give out Under had been my socks, and I spent most of my time there with uncomfortable bare feet against the seams of my shoes (that slowly got a bit too tight—there was no way to fix or replace them). I still remembered how my feet hurt after the long overnight walk over the state border, from the Factory in Maine to here. I still get a huge silly smile on my face when I walk into Riverport's shoe store.

The socks were warm.

The doctor here had listened gravely when I told him I was always cold. He couldn't find anything wrong, made some mild suggestions in that almost grandmotherly way of his, then last Christmas he gave me this pair of socks—that he'd knitted with his own hands.

"Warm heart," he'd said. Mine felt like a stone left out through a winter's night.

He'd met the first six of us early in our first year here, agreed to help us, agreed to help all of us sight unseen; but the first, terrible year had brought him especially close to those of us who got out early. He was around now, occasionally, putting together medical information for the lawsuit. He was the doctor to those of us who didn't want to try explaining the drug (or who it had stuck us with) to anyone else. He was the one helping my wife and me, suggesting the whole system with the thermometer and calendar and explaining to both of us why it was important.

I'd heard, but I'd seen in his eyes that he knew it wouldn't do any good, no more than it would for most of the rest of us. He'd tried to catch me in conversations when I ran into him at company holiday dinners or smaller gatherings. He was always the soul of tact and politeness—I guess he always remembered us as exhausted, undernourished striplings, half-mad with being over-stressed. He always tried to get at how I was feeling, whether I was low, was I fully enjoying the life I had now—was I taking vacations? Was I making time for just me and her? Was it still an effort to finish meals? Was it still difficult to get a full night's sleep? How were the nightmares?

If Quin were here, he'd say something black like, "they say hello."

The doctor meant all of this as a friend; you could just see how anyone's suffering from Under (and its consequences) twisted his sense of what was right and fair and good. He helped the boys just the same as he'd help women in the same straits, referring them to what help there was, talking to them—really doing whatever he could for all of us so that successful lawsuit or no we'd all have the apt revenge of a good and full life Above.

I wondered what he'd suffered to care so much; or maybe that's what made men doctors instead of accountants.

Oh God, I'd have to apologize to each and every one of my friends I'd yelled at tonight.

My wife came in and went thought her bedtime routine. I did my best to fall asleep early.

She got under the covers and ran her hand down the length of my flannel-covered side.

"I can get you my aunt's fur coat out of the hallway closet."

"I've been cold all day," I said, in a tone that was too much of a petulant whine.

"Emran."

I didn't like that tone of voice, but I did everything possible never to get angry at her.

"Yes, baby?" I said, sitting up and looking at her.

"You've never called me 'baby' before."

I smiled. "I can start." My heart ached for the love-names Tarquin had called me, which I'd never told her.

"Emran, I know you were in a hurry to help out at your cousin's, but when you have to leave like that write me a note."

"Next time," I said with a sinking heart that I tried not to show on my face.

"And you're upset about something."

I sighed. "I lost my temper with an old friend of mine. I'm going to have to tell him I'm sorry tomorrow."

"Why?"

I tried to think of what I could honestly tell her.

"Well, he's always been a prankster, and he said something about how long it's taking us to start a family."

"Does *he* have a wife?"

"No, actually." I forced myself to smile as if amused by her point, as if consoled for the friend's slight, "but I yelled at him and Sam had to come in to make the peace."

"Sam knows this fellow?"

I nodded, silently counting how many people I had ever mentioned to her in connection with Sam's. The Factory and the drug didn't naturally follow from my cousin's restaurant, but I must be careful that nothing will let her put all of us or anything about our common past Under together.

"So did your friend apologize to *you*? Do I know this friend of yours?" She looked ready to say a tart word to him.

"No, Em, I don't think you've ever met him. He's just a guy that works at Sam's—a dark haired fellow with brown eyes. I don't think you've seen him around town." I mentioned Charles Ray, an old actor Marcus looked somewhat like. My wife shook her head. "Anyway, you're right. He didn't apologize to me at all. I think he's just jealous."

"Not much luck with the girls?"

"No," I said with a straight face, "not much luck at all."

She settled back against the pillows. "Well it's either looks or personality. If he's any kind of handsome, then he must not be too nice a fellow, after all."

I reminded myself not to say that my old boyfriend was handsome, and I worried I'd said too much about what he looked like.

"Well, a lot of these guys are hard-luck cases with troubles of their own: can't keep a job, troubled marriages, bad tempers. My cousin Sam's a kind guy, gives a job to hard-luck cases…that's probably why he gets shorthanded sometimes. He doesn't exactly hire the most reliable men in the world," I said, starting to feel a bit sleepy.

I'd trusted these 119 men with my life—they could have just turned me over to the police and waved, as it was very, very obvious that only I had killed Quin. Instead they've all kept my secrets, and a small core of them showed up in court, served as witnesses, came up with (and swore to) all the lies I told to make it look like I killed Quin out of self-defense.

"You're nice to say you're sorry to him."

"What?" I said, starting slightly.

"You're nice to tell that friend you're sorry when he picked on you first."

I nodded. A thought slowly crossed my mind:

"Emily, I'm sorry I left you alone all night, you must have been worried."

"Oh, I figured you were alright—that you'd gone on a late errand, or out for a drive to clear your head, or you'd forgotten something at work." She laughed a little. "You know, you smelled like flowers when you first came in. Did you buy me something?"

What had I done with the bag? Would I need to buy her something, early tomorrow, as a cover? It was still in the car, right on the passenger seat, and I'd agreed to drop her off at— no, I'd thrown it out in the trash, outside, as I'd come in the house.

"Can't remember?"

"Now I do…I was working in the prep kitchen and someone had brought in all the flowers for the tables, I was working right next to them." This wasn't so, but everyone would know to nod and say, "I guess so, Mrs. Greene. It was pretty busy that night," if she ever asked. We protected each other's secrets.

Or I hoped we still did. Oh God I've got to treat my old friends better. Any one of them could knock on our front door and tell her things, show her the grave, newspaper clippings, tell her things about our past that would turn her whole world upside down.

"Hey sleepy, I know this gown isn't as nice as my summer one.…" She settled in a way that made her best features dance.

I smiled fondly, and you'd think having sex would be the perfect thing for how I felt, but I was still full of the kind of cold that made me want to curl up under blankets in an armchair alone. Or with someone in all innocence, as only a source of warmth. I wanted a sunny window, or the wood stove at Terry's place, or the arrival of a whole 'nother season. I was more sleepy than frustrated, exhausted really, and I shook my head.

"I'm sorry, you look great…."

She looked hurt around the edges. "The schedule is a suggestion, you know—not a requirement. It won't hurt for us to 'try more often.'"

I took her arms so she couldn't turn away.

"Emily, please." I took a page from Clem: "Every morning when I wake up I'm glad I married you, and every morning I choose you, and this, as the best life I could ever, ever have." That's how I'd felt about Quin, but this cheered her. "You will be the mother of our daughter," I added.

She laughed, saying, "How do you know it'll be a girl?"

"You will—and you are the only woman I could ever marry." That was true, and so was the rest, "I wasn't kind enough to you today, I'm sorry, I'll try to do better tomorrow. Think of it this way—what would you like to do with the money I made today at Sam's? Is there something special? Something extra?" I smiled.

She used to enjoy that game, and I'd enjoyed dreaming up things to surprise her with or little gestures to make— something I could never do with Quin since all our money was held in common, and with the bond he'd know what surprise I was thinking of as soon as the idea crossed my mind. The memory made me smile, anyway.

My wife did not melt; she still looked a little hurt. I wished I *could* read her mind: I never knew whether being more placating and kind helped or only irritated her more. I never knew if I should just leave her alone or whether that seemed cruel. I did love her—and everything that's ordinary and successful about my life depended on her, and on this baby. I kissed her forehead. She turned over and turned off the lamp. I held her close and said kind things, as if to a hurt boyfriend Under. I hadn't had anything to give them, either, but my time and attention (when I could spare it during all the pretending) and maybe a bit of extra desert or a small handful of stolen chocolate chips.

The things and the money didn't charm her anymore. Now that we have everything just so, she wants to keep it that way, aside from updating the curtains or the plates every few years. Tarquin and I hung towels until we could finish sewing mismatched yards into crude curtains, and we borrowed our plates from friends' yard sale finds. I'd hear about it from Emily if we had to do without, or had anything less than our current situation, but I'd never been able to explain to her why giving her little gifts and surprises meant so much to me.

In a sleepy pause she said to me, "I was all right this evening, Em: I finished that stripe on the afghan." Her hair had the too-sweet smell of expensive shampoo; I could not tell any difference from the inexpensive brand she used when we first met.

"The burgundy one?"

Her skin, her gown, the sheets smelled like all the brands in a women's magazine; I missed the simple lemon smell of the laundry soap Quin and I had used, the clean smell of the cheap soap and shampoo we bought. I used them until Emily took over the grocery shopping, laughing at my bachelor frugality. I suddenly missed how Quin smelled; Emily always smelled like something that came out of a bottle. I'm not sure how a human being could do that.

"You noticed," her voice carried the tone of a pleased smile.

"Did you have enough yarn? Do you want a new color? When I go to the business meetings at the restaurant, all I have to do after I say my bit is watch the doctor knit."

"He knits?" She sounded shocked, as she should be. In this world, men didn't knit, or cook, or help with the housework, or take not becoming fathers as the least of their problems. Men didn't have boyfriends, or set up house with each other, or kiss on the mouth to say "hello" and "goodbye," or exchange tokens of eternal fidelity (be they of cloth or gold), or fall in love with each other. I loved Quin; I can't push that off on the drug. I loved Quin, and I still do.

I felt warm all over. I sat up to peel back a layer of blankets.

"The doctor knits: he knits for premature babies and for unmarried mothers and their children. He made me these socks. Anyway, you can imagine how bored I get at those meetings that I pay that much attention."

"Why is he at business meetings for the restaurant?"

I tried my catch-all answer: "Dunno," I mumbled. "Medical insurance?" I ventured as a false guess.

"And I thought he was such a nice man," she muttered with a small frown in her voice, clearly finding him peculiar. "Are you sure he's—"

I shrugged. "He's not married to that nurse who watches the desk for him."

My wife giggled a little. "I know, she was telling me about the present her latest boyfriend gave her. She is such a…well, if she were a man, I'd call her a playboy," Emily shook her head a bit against her pillow. "Well I guess that's why he can work around women all day," she said with a note of disgusted pity.

"Why does knitting for sick little babies make him a nancy? All you need to knit are two hands with five fingers—"

"Honestly, Em. It makes him the only thing he could be. It's a disgusting topic: I thought he was such a nice man, too."

"Do you want to change doctors?" I said into the silence.

"No, now I know for certain he won't look at me that way. That's a nice feeling, considering what we're going to him for. You must feel crawly, though."

I'd never had the least sense that the doctor was anything but professional with all of us. And she didn't know it, but he'd already taken samples of everything that didn't require dissection from us. That's how we know (after almost a decade Above) that we're almost as saturated with the drug as we were when we left the Factory: it's why I'm so careful with her. I have to hold everything I feel at arm's length, which I didn't when I was with Quin.… I made myself not think of him. I put my mind back on our conversation.

"No, Emily, I don't feel odd at all. He's a good doctor: that's all that matters. So do you want me to drop you off at that yarn store, tomorrow?"

She settled placidly against her pillow. "No, Em, I'll get more yarn for the afghan cheaply at a rummage sale one weekend or another—or I think Agnes said she has more than she knows what to do with from that sweater she started that drove her crazy. I can swap her something I don't like out of my basket or bring her a cake—" she yawned— "or a pie."

"Who's it for, the afghan?"

My wife laughed a little under her breath. I think she meant me; it's too big and all the wrong colors for a baby. Most of the things she knits are from boutique-bought yarn—it felt lovely but I never knew yarn could be that expensive.

I let out a breath.

There's nothing I could make her—except a mother. And after that I was out of cards.

Was this it? Was this the rest of my life? Oh God, I never owed Quin anything, yet I took everything from him. What had I gotten myself into—and why in the blazes did I feel the same panic I felt about being bonded?

I was not, now, and I chose this life freely. I loved her, and no one could suspect anything perverted or criminal about me now. This was what I thought my future would be, Under (when I dared dream about things turning out right). There was nothing wrong with my life now, and I was better off than the first dozen co-workers I could name. Clem had no choice in his bond: I'm sure he tells himself they're happy. But how could they possibly be happy? I can think of many reasons why he and my old boyfriend were an unlikely match (from old habit Under I made myself not fume over this). Marcus enjoyed his freedom—as had I.

"Goodnight, Em," I said softly, but she was asleep, making a slight snore with every breath. I turned over and settled on my side of the bed, not touching her, wishing I were alone in my own bunk. I took off the robe and messed with the blankets until I had pulled one sheet and a thin coverlet over me—our long-sleeved uniforms were all we had to sleep in Under, and each bunk only had one set of sheets and a single blanket. I settled down, pleasantly cool. I'd left the bedroom window cracked open to let the steam from the shower out. It felt about 55 degrees, which my wife didn't mind under all her blankets. She was safe. She was protected. She was sound asleep.

I was safe, too. Nothing was going to disrupt this life I'd put together, now, nothing would take apart this home, this marriage, this family-to-be. Nothing would endanger my job or my place in the world of outsiders; nothing would take away my car or my house or empty my bank accounts. I wouldn't do anything crazy any longer; I hadn't after killing Quin. Everyone would brush off that rash of temper I had tonight. We all got temperamental with the drug. I had a right life, a good life I was happy with. Everything would be fine after we had the baby.

The mistakes I made with Quin won't happen again. I will never have to look up at a gray, cold prison ceiling and wonder where all the good things in my life slipped off to and why it was all my fault.

The worst thing I have to do in my life is make an appointment with the barber (and the mechanic). I didn't have to apologize to all those friends—they taunted me, they provoked me, they were cruel and deserved every word of what I said to them. I won't go back there again until I have to, and if I see them on the street, I'll ignore them.

Goddamned pansies.

Emily and I will have a baby. It'll prove I made the right choice—it's nothing any of them can do. My love is better than theirs, I've got it better in every way than any of them: none of them have a new coat or a new car or a new furnace or….

I fell asleep while making that happy list.

A warm touch woke me, only the furnace trying to compensate for the window I'd stupidly left open. The heating bill would be a killer… I opened my eyes. A tall pale figure stood by the window—only the white thin undercurtain billowed out by the night air. I shut my eyes, safe and contented, ignoring it. I've had enough nightmares enough nights that nothing can scare me, no matter what I open my eyes to. I've never sat up in bed, wild with fear.

The weight of someone sitting down on the edge of the bed. My wife snored from a few feet away. The sound of fingers worrying a small piece of cloth, and a gentle hand took my hurt wrist and began to rub the soreness out of it.

A patient sigh.

A gently arch voice said, "is now any better than Under? You were always cold—and pretending—there, too. They're very much alike: you're dreaming about then and sleepwalking through now."

"I'm happy now, Quin," I said in a cold voice. "There's nothing I can do about it."

"Yes you can: you can apologize to who you've hurt, both Under and Above. You can be honest: where's the young man who couldn't wait to be honest if God ever let him see his friends again? Where's the young man who wanted everyone to know we were bonded? How did you get so ashamed and so angry?"

I didn't answer him.

"This woman did nothing to you, and you're keeping her here with false smiles and bribes like some half-willing boyfriend. You're acting like a man, and you've pushed away that you were ever a boy—a human being capable of tenderness or being hurt."

I cut in on him. "I can go to church on Sundays if I want a sermon, Quin."

"Short form: you've got to be weak to be strong. One night a man will come to you in a fit, the door will be locked, and no one will be able to hear you. He bears a gift in brutal form: what you do will determine whether he kills you, whether he shatters all this life you have, or whether your acceptance will tear off the dark wrappings and show you the most golden thing you've ever known."

"Can't you just take me to a graveyard and show me my own headstone?" I said acidly.

"You want to fight," Quin said fondly. "How sweet. No, Beloved: you were just there." There was a silence as if he was thinking or looking around the room. "Actually, there's no saving this life: it's brittle. It's all made of ice. Anyone but you could see right through it." He looked at my wife for a moment, watching her sleep. "Sleep without dreams, Aiden," he said and bent close. "Tomorrow's just another day."

I started up in bed: that had been a kiss, a moist, warm, real kiss. No, it was just a memory from earlier today; this was my bed, my wife was asleep beside me, this was my house, my car was out in the driveway. I got up and shut the window without looking at the weather: it was cold, and it would be goddamned fucking cold until the end of time.

Epilogue: A Bit After Midnight

Marcus was standing on my lawn. He was looking at the ground for something small to throw at this window. I made myself not swear at him (which would wake up the neighbors—and my wife); I grabbed my coat and went out to him.

I suddenly felt like I was Under again, a boy among boys, a man among men.

"Did you see anyone? At the window?"

"You," he replied, smiling despite the turmoil on his face, "Emran—"

"Will you leave me alone? Will you leave me and my marriage and my life fucking alone?"

He backed away a little, his hands up in a peacemaking gesture.

"Could I interest you in some introspection? Or at least some advice?"

"You're here to take this away from me!"

"Trust me, I don't want it: I'm bonded." He bit off saying something more and ventured, "Can you tell how mad you are?"

"You made me—get out of here before I finish what I started!"

He began to back up, slowly, and a dark car at the street's edge whined into gear from neutral and came up to meet him.

"Get in," Sam said to Marcus, softly, in a tone that implied there was no call for being a hero just now. Neither Marcus nor Clem owned a car: no one I saw tonight did; the ancient red wreck wheezing exhaust on my front walk belonged to the restaurant. Sam and Marcus must have been going to put the till in the bank's night drop. Sam didn't look at me or speak to me; either a man's shaming me for letting the drug make me so mad and causing trouble, or the simple sense that anything would provoke me just now.

Marcus seemed to calculate for a moment: he'd escaped several rapes and quite a few beatings (although not all of either) Under. He seemed to be weighing his ability to dodge against the value of sending me to jail for an assault charge. But we try to avoid explaining ourselves to the police and work everything out among ourselves, which is why a prompt apology is so important.

That was an afterthought. All I could think at the moment was how he'd taunted and mocked me and how he deserved what he'd get when my fists connected with him.

And how good that would feel, how good each blow would feel as it landed.

"Sound familiar?" An arch voice observed.

No one else turned, but I froze: that's how my last fit with Quin had felt.

Marcus murmured a prayer of thanks under his breath and was inside the car in one step. Sam pulled away smoothly, rolling—the car fought going into the correct gear.

"No one can do anything for him," my old boss's voice murmured. "He'll just have to sort this out himself."

Whatever else he—or they—said was lost as the car went into gear, jumped a little, and ambled to the end of the block. The engine purred, and Sam switched the headlamps on as the car disappeared around the corner.

I felt tired and confused, my mind too prone to lazy tangents about my old (former?) friends and things that had happened Under.

"You're going to tell me to go to bed," I said softly to the empty yard.

"You could lie down and cut everyone's misery short," Tarquin said, in the tone of someone looking thoughtfully up at the winter night, "but you'll live twice double what I did—don't worry, Beloved, most of it will be better than this."

I didn't move.

"Go in, I can't touch you when you're wide awake," he said.

I missed him terribly. "Is that what you're doing, trying to seduce me?"

A deeply sarcastic silence.

"Will you think about what you're saying, Aiden, for just one moment? Will you look at what you've done? You're saying you're sorry: believe me, you will need these men's help, one day. This is all going to shatter—don't slam the door."

He said it in a tone of voice that wasn't reprimand, but that understood my anger, that understood me (better than anyone since ever has), and considerate of the woman in my bed…simply because Tarquin was far more thoughtful and sincere than anyone would believe. I knew everything he felt for a nearly a year; he was only arch with people he thought should know better than what they were doing….

I carefully got back into bed. My wife was sound asleep.

"Beloved?" I breathed softly. He'd always called me by my middle name; I didn't let anyone else do so after his death—even though the fellows who'd gotten out early all began to call me that because of him.

"Hm?" My wife said.

"It was just a dream." This is what is real, this bed, this house, the baby we will have. I couldn't pull close to her; I tried and just wanted to be alone. God I felt cold. I'd shut the window, hadn't I?

I wanted to get my square of cloth from work; I'd held it and cried on it in the months after his murder. It helped a little; all we can figure is that the bond is the drug passed back and forth between the same two bodies: by tears of joy, by the sweat of being together, by the saliva of full kisses, by....

I sighed. What a disgusting life that had been. I looked back and couldn't believe I did any of that, with him, with Marcus, with any of the rest. No, this was what a man should do (and soon I'd have the baby to prove it).

"You're sick," Quin murmured, an earth-cool hand on my forehead.

"Why am I so cold?"

"Same reason."

"Tell me something nice," I said petulantly.

"You'll get better," he said. "As soon as you can be honest—you could be honest with me, Beloved. Was this worth that—after what you went through Under?"

"Go back to your earth, back to that bed I made you, and sleep until sunrise—aren't you supposed to leave by dawn?"

"It's not dawn, yet—it won't be daybreak for a while," he said, as archly as ever.

"Fuck off," I muttered into my pillow.

The moment his hand left mine I felt colder than any day Under.

It was dark, I was alone in bed, another day of lying and pretending ahead of me in too few hours, after another over-long workday. I curled up shivering, buried under ground, wondering when the hell it would be spring.

Author Biography

A Day in Deep Freeze was originally written for the 3-Day Novel Contest.

Lisa Shapter attended Earlham College in Indiana and the Bread Loaf Young Writers' Conference (now the New England Young Writers' Conference) in Vermont. She was apprenticed to an ABAA antiquarian book dealer and has worked for Wesleyan University Press and the Johns Hopkins University Press. She lives in New England where she writes a short story each week, collects antique typewriters, and researches the history of women in SF.

Her interconnected fiction uses the perspectives of multiple narrators, each with their own truths, half-truths, and shortfalls. Although each of her novellas and short stories stands on its own, each is part of a larger story told across several pieces that develops facets and shadows under different narrators' perspectives. Her LBGT-friendly feminist military SF has appeared in *Black Denim Lit, Expanded Horizons, Four Star Stories, Kaleidotrope*, and in the *M-Brane SF* anthology *Things We Are Not*.